I0735331

Time Will Tell

A Monstrous Story

Dinah Roseberry

This is a work of fiction.

Names, characters, businesses, places, events, or incidents are either the products of the author's imagination or used in a fictitious manner. Any resemblance to actual person, living or dead, or actual events is purely coincidental.

Time Will Tell
A Monstrous Story

PROLOG
A MARRIAGE UPSET

She radiated beauty to anyone near enough to see her. Her princess-white gown was tailored to fit her tightly across the bodice and through the waist. Tiny pedals of yellow and blue flowers at its hem appeared to move in the soft breeze like the soft wings of butterflies. The sun shining down on her veil seemed to make it sparkle, and her delicate hands, though trembling, projected daylight as though a sizzling of innocence came directly from her fingertips.

But her insides crawled with loathing and fear. He was everything she did not want in a husband: ugly and sinister of heart, full of false affection and hatred—and further, his hideous family would see evil forever touching all living beings and things throughout the world because of this unholy union. It was a horror what she was doing. Yet if she didn't do it, *all* life would be destroyed. But why did it have to be her? Why now? Why, when she was so young and so full of life and dreams? This was something she would not wish on anyone. She couldn't give away or bid this horrible duty to another. She gritted her teeth and fought the scream that was hoovering in her throat. *It's my duty; it's my duty,* she kept reassuring herself in her swirling mind.

Still, though she wanted that scream to bellow throughout the lands, she stood silent, knowing that she would be forced to stomach this marriage or to run for the rest of her life—which would be an eternity. Eternity was a very long time for one so young. She'd just turned 16. Though she knew that, in her heart, fleeing the situation would feel so right, she'd considered it and then dismissed it. Oh yes, that running might be worth the pain and anguish—the finality of spending her life with this cruel man—she'd finally given in for her family's sake. That path would be temporary at best and most likely worse when she was caught. And she would be caught—eventually. So, she would marry this man. She did not allow herself to think about what that would mean at the very basest of levels. She couldn't face that in this minute of sorrow.

That would be something for another day. Another hour. Another minute. She shivered in repulsion.

Calling him a man was a stretch in her eyes—and to all who saw him (outside his own relatives). The man was not a man. He was not a person. He was a monster—one that knew nothing but devastation and wicked force. He was ugly in his soul and on his face, and in his mind. Just a look from his dead eyes struck terror into the mild-mannered ways of "normal" folk. As for marriage, there was—nor could there ever be—any kind of love around this monstrous being. No love. No emotion that applied to a real girl. Not for her—or any future woman for that matter. She bit down on the feelings of resentment she was experiencing at being in this position yet again. Would life never change for her?

The sheer, white veil hid the tears falling steadily down her cheeks from her valued and loved family standing outside the dark castle with the horrendous clan of her husband-to-be. There was no sense letting them see again the conflict of her situation. They understood enough. Seeing it would be to put more torture on their souls. Two families stood face to face on either side of the stone pathway, one sad and horror stricken, the other grinning with sly meanness, because they realized they had the upper hand in the deal. Both sides knew, however, that a time of change was coming. Whether good or bad, a new life cycle was about to begin, and both felt the need for it to succeed—whatever the circumstances or sacrifices. It truly was a matter of life and death.

The girl sucked in her breath and pushed all the fear from her mind that she could. There was no hope for her...but maybe her family would triumph. She sighed. Maybe they would find a way this time to defeat the evil. She offered a soft prayer to the Creator. "Please help me," she whispered. "I've always done what was to be done for the worlds. For you. Don't leave me now to this horrible ending."

A sudden commotion at the castle gates disturbed her prayers, and it drew her attention from her immediate problems. It was then that she saw him: the one. Her one! She knew in an instant that this young man was her salvation and her lover for all time. He was the one she had been waiting for these last months of abusive courtship. The Creator had not abandoned her!

Goose flesh jumped to her skin, and she fought a shiver that would tip off those around her that her dreams were coming to life. She could feel energy flash in her eyes—if, indeed, this new spicy sense was a thing of feeling or flashing!

This man would save her from the monster that would be her spouse. She knew it. She felt it. She tasted his strength deep in her soul. He had finally come, even though she'd feared the worst after the last time. The last time...she banished the thoughts. He was here. Now. No time to dwell in what had happened before. This was different!

Did she, however, dare risk the wrath of the Creator? Was her happiness and the banishment of evil to the world enough to change the fates? It hadn't been before. Had the Creator really considered the prayers of a 16-year-old girl? Was she mistaken that she had the backing of the powerful one?

Was this the time? Now? In this place? She quietly drew in her breath. She thought so. It *had* to be so. She replaced the hidden tears with a soft smile beneath the veil. Her heart pounded and thoughts in her brain rushed.

The fight was on.

Her great white knight stepped forward...again...

Let the battle against good against evil begin!

1
THE JOB

How many times had Lucas ran through the dream in the past week? It seemed that he couldn't even fall asleep in front of the television without a strange delusion these days. Not that he was complaining. The dreams were great—so real and full of adventure—and always in a new place, in some other time. This was certainly better than his school's history class with lectures that were sleep inducing for sure.

There was a truly odd thing about the dreams though. There was a girl in each one who seemed the same every time. Sometimes her hair was a different color or length, her skin tone could change, and her voice held different inflections—but she was still the same girl. Her face had a delicate strength, and her eyes held a spark of energy he'd not seen before. He was sure this was the same girl.

"Luke!" cried his mother from what sounded like a long way off. "Hurry up! You'll be late!"

He could hear his mother, but not clearly. It was as though something was interfering with the sounds in the house—like he was in two places at one time. That was certainly the strangest thing he'd ever felt. What was happening to him?

In seconds, his mother was blocked out completely and he was in total darkness...not the kind of darkness that happens at night when he went to sleep, but like something sinister happening when he was wide awake. Something crazed. Something watching. Lucas's head lifted up and he made a full turn away from his mother's voice. There was a tiny light where the bedroom door should have been, but the rest of his room was gone. Was he losing consciousness? His mind?

He called out to his mother for help, but the words coming from his mouth were swallowed up by the world he'd found himself in. Fear started to grip him. It was then he saw her face again. The girl. The one he'd been dreaming about. She looked scared—that couldn't be good. He stared at her closely through the black space. It was as though he was looking at a painting on a wall, with the paints dripping down and disappearing into the darkness. She was not real, yet she had all the real features and hints of a girl he could really care about. And how could that be possible in a place where he really wasn't?

Then she was gone, and his mother voice slammed into his brain like a bullet might, had he been inside one of his video games. "Lucas! Did you hear me? You're going to be late, and you have to eat before you go!" She was serious—steam coming out of the ears serious.

He took in his breath and forcefully dismissed what he'd just seen. He'd think about it later. He was in no state of mind now to further that particular scenario. He did not want to ever be in a dark place like that. Girl or no girl. And it wasn't real anyway. Not in any...real...sense...

"I'm here," he yelled out to his mom, running down the stairs, two at a time, and slipping onto the breakfast barstool. "And I have plenty of time. Not due in till nine."

"Well, it's eight thirty now, as the clock on the wall tells us in no uncertain terms." She blew a strand of brown hair from her eyes and straight up into the air as she placed a plate on the bar in front of him. "And I hope you just don't forget how hard your father has worked at the Bellington and what an opportunity he's given you. There were other boys older than you applying for that job. And you got it."

With her hands on her hips and dark reminding eyes, she looked just like a volcano ready to erupt into a speech. The thought made him smile and then cringe—how he hated lectures of any kind. "Just don't you forget how that job offer came about," she said, pointing at his plate. "Now eat your eggs."

Lucas smiled and rolled his eyes. He never worried about his mother's quick temper. She was a great lady, and he did his best not to upset her. He could do worse in the mother field.

Very calmly, he put down his fork and winked at her. "Ma, the hotel's only across the street and down the road a bit. I'll be early. And don't worry. You've reminded me a hundred times that Dad was the one who got me this summer job. And yes, I also remember that I'm only sixteen and that lots of other college guys applied and lost out."

"Don't get smart with me," said his mother, but she was more playful now. She grabbed a kitchen towel from the counter and snapped the air near his stool. "I just want you to do a good job. Looks good on a college application."

Lucas nodded, blew her an exaggerated kiss, and ate his eggs.

"Ma?" he said when he was finished eating, "do we have any nuts in our family?"

"Nuts?" she questioned, her eyebrows wrinkling.

"Yeah, you know, crazies. Looneys."

"Just you," she said and added with a grumble, "and I wish you had time to help me wash the breakfast dishes. Why do you ask about crazies?"

"I'm serious," he said. "Do we have any nuts in our family?"

His mother wiped her hands on the dishtowel over her shoulder and looked thoughtfully at Lucas. "No, honey. We do not have any nuts in our family. Now, what's this all about? You look serious."

Lucas sighed and looked down at his empty plate. The yellow egg remnants blended into the spring pattern of ducks that were also yellow. Creepy. Who bought dishes like that? Mothers certainly did have some nuts in them whether they knew it or not.

"Well, it's just that there's been some strange stuff going on in my life lately, and it's kinda weird. I thought maybe I might've inherited some kind of mental illness or something. That stuff's hereditary you know."

"What kind of strange stuff, Lucas?" She looked worried now, and she slid down onto a stool across the counter from him.

"Nothing specific really," he replied and then glanced over at his mother's face. She was giving him a questioning mothers-know-everything-so-don't-even-try-to-hide-something stare. He swallowed hard and slowly continued, "Actually...I've been having these dreams lately."

"Oh," said his mother, relieved. She sighed and moved back to the sink where she resumed the dishes. "Everyone has odd dreams at times, dear," she said over her shoulder to him. "That's nothing to worry about. It's your brain rattling around in there trying to make sense of your day. Nothing wrong. Just annoying from time to time."

"I guess you're right," he agreed, "but there's also something else." Lucas paused, wondering whether it was a good idea to tell her. This would surely sound crazy and he didn't need his mother pawing over him. She was a great mom and all, but at times, the gooey stuff just gave him the willies.

"At the hotel, in the elevator...well, you know I've been hanging around there lately with Todd and all...and in the elevator there..." Lucas stopped and gritted his teeth. "Well, it gets kind of foggy in there sometimes. In the elevator that is."

"I'm sure that's from people smoking, dear. Nasty habit. And they're not supposed to do it in the elevators. It's a state thing, I believe. But I know they do it—I can smell it sometimes. People are rude. You should report it. Secondhand smoking can destroy your lungs, and firsthand smoking, in case you ever think about taking that up, will cause cancer lickety-split." She continued to scrub dishes and began nodding. "I'm glad you never started that. You'll thank us one day for pushing that piece of advice down your throat."

He rolled his eyes at her back. "Yeah, yeah, I know. But it's not smoke, Ma. It's fog swirling around, and it only happens when I'm alone. Or, at least so far I've been alone."

Lucas's mother turned and looked hard at him with a frown that aged her ten years around the eyes. "That's nonsense, Lucas. It's smoke. You should report it. There's no fog in elevators. There could be something wrong with it though. There's that to think about, I guess. Report it." She turned back to the dirty dishes in the sink. It was evident that her answer was final.

Lucas frowned, too, knowing she had dismissed him and what he felt was an important problem—even if no one else thought so. It was a feeling. A strong one, too. He carried his plate to his mother without comment. Then he grabbed the lightweight Bellington Hotel jacket from the hall closet, deciding that parents weren't really the best people to confide weird stuff to anyway. What had he been thinking?

"I guess I'm off," he said, kissing her lightly on the cheek. It was a gesture that was difficult for him to remember. But he found that in the long run, it kept his mother calm. When she was calm, he had more freedom. So, parent kissing could work well in most circumstances. He smiled at her, too, as an extra added effect. "And I'll be a whole ten minutes early, Ma!"

"Don't be smart!" she snapped. Then her voice softened. "Luke, don't worry about that smoke thing. Or the dreams. Dreams are nothing but your mind getting rid of the day's rubbish, and the smoke could be coming from the machinery or something. Maybe you should have maintenance take a look at the elevator. Maybe there's a weight factor involved. A certain amount of weight might make the thing off balance or something. That could cause the thing to smoke, right?"

"Maybe," he said and smiled at her. "Anyway, don't worry. I'm fine."

With that, Lucas walked from the small two-story row home, across the street and down the road to the old Bellington Hotel.

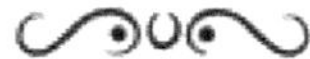

In front of the hotel, Lucas took a moment to look at the building in the bright morning sunlight. It really was quite striking—for a building. There wasn't even one piece of graffiti on it. His father, who was head of Hotel Management, had said the old hotel had been built in 1910. A horn blasted from a passing car that nearly hit him, even though he was in a crosswalk and following the signs. It snapped Lucas back to the present, a finger gesture almost lashing out at the aggressive driver. Instead, he shrugged, thinking that the best way to handle fools was to ignore them and get on with the day. Parental advice was good from time to time. He continued across the street and into the hotel.

Looking around with awe, Lucas gave a deep sigh. He was amazed—as he was every time he found himself inside the hotel—at the enormous lobby. Only a church could do it better. A really big church! Decorated in the richest reds of the 1900s, the old building was a page from a history book with high regal ceilings, old antique furnishings, and architectural elements. And clean. A bit too clean perhaps, he always thought. But *clean* was the word of the day these days. Though all kinds of people visited, it held the air of aristocratic elegance, almost questioning those who didn't hold some sort of high power as to their even belonging in such a grand place. He certainly felt like he was a small cog in the wheel that was the Bellington.

The elevator was straight ahead on the far side of the lobby, but Lucas hesitated to report his findings inside that strange boxlike contraption. That was the elevator. A chill made its way up his spine, forcing him to gaze about the room and away from the device. Instead, he let his mind wander to his first encounter with it.

Upon initially being interviewed for the morning shift job at the Bellington, Lucas had been surprised to learn that the original elevator was still being used for transporting guests to and from the four floors of the hotel. His now-good friend, Todd Coral, had taught him how to work the old-time machine—and old-time seemed a polite description for the clanking, creaking thing. This had been late the previous week—without pay, of course. Todd, with his shocking stand-up-straight-even-without-hair-stuff hair, was an underpaid busboy for the hotel, who seemed to have had his hand in the running of every department at one time or another. His father, head of maintenance, saw to it that his son had a job of sorts each summer from the time Todd had turned twelve. Sixteen years old now, as was Lucas, Todd had served, in one way or another, in every department from housekeeping to kitchen and even accounting (though that had been a short stint, math not being a strong suit).

The first time he had shown Lucas the elevator had been interesting. The machine was a marvel. There was a long handle, waist level, controlling the starting and stopping, and the operator had to have a real good feel for when to use that handle. It moved in a half circle, left to right and back. For the few rides in the beginning, Lucas was forced to have his passengers step a foot up or a foot down to exit. Tips were slow coming because of his poor timing. But he'd thought that tips anyway were a plus no matter how few. He'd never heard of people tipping in elevators, but they sure did in this hotel. This was a very good thing.

He had gotten better at working the handle, though, with practice. When the bell sounded in his tiny cubicle by the elevator, lighting up the floor needing him, he would hop into the mirrored box and shoot up to the appropriate floor. Then he would slowly take the elevator up or down for the guest, hoping that his now good timing, big smile, and pleasant manner might earn him a dollar tip—or more, if a big spender was aboard. Lucas didn't like getting quarters, but it *was* what it was, and people spent what they would.

Lucas sighed, his attention pulled from the past to the elevator before him this morning. He could see the doors close at the opposite end of the lobby. No one was working the controls. And fog was swirling slowly above the floor inside and slipping out into the lobby as the metal doors slid shut. He *had* to be seeing things. There was no other explanation, especially since everyone else seemed oblivious to it.

Then something made him think of the dreams. A shiver carried him forward. He wondered if he was having a premonition of some kind. Dreams. Foggy elevators. Can't be good, he thought. "No, no, this cannot be good."

2

REAL BUT NOT REAL

Todd looked at Lucas with sarcastic raised eyebrows. "You *are* kidding, right?"

"No. I'm not kidding. I swear; I'm not making this up!"

"I'm gone need another Coke if you're actually expecting me to believe this," remarked Todd, sliding the lid from the Styrofoam cooler and twisted the cap from the Coca-Cola bottle. "Start from the beginning," he said after a long cold swig. "I can't believe you've been feeling this nuts and still keepin' it from me."

"That's the whole point. It really *is* nuts. And I really didn't want people to think I was crazier than I already am. Even you. I mean, there's no way you're gone believe me. My own mother treated me like a little kid this morning."

Todd merely raised his eyebrows again in a look that said no surprise there and reached for the chips.

"Okay," began Lucas, "first it was the dreams. I've been having them for at least two weeks. Terrific dreams about this girl." He paused, allowing the image of her to flow back to his mind. "She's always different, but always the same somehow."

"Right," responded Todd, drinking again from the bottle and passing it to Lucas. "Makes sense so far. There's a girl in a dream who's the same, but different."

Lucas frowned. "It's hard to explain. She always looks the same to some degree. But her hair changes. And her face some. Even the skin tone is different each time. But she's the same. There's a look in her eyes. Deep inside, sort of. And her voice is always the same—soft and . . . and . . . well, she's perfect," he said, his voice drifting quietly off.

"Okay, so she's perfect," said Todd with a grunt, his mouth full of chips. "So's Melissa Carolson in our history class, but you don't see me all upset cuz I dream about *her* every night. It's what we do." Todd's eyes hardened. "You're getting sand all over the blanket. And I can't stand sand in my suit. It gets mixed up with the gooey suntan oil."

Lucas ignored his friend's remarks. "I'm telling you, Todd, this is different. The dreams are *real*. Not fantasy, but real things happening to me."

"Okay. So far, we got the same but different and fantasy that's real. Doin' just fine. Let's skip this part and get to the time travel stuff," Todd suggested and began whistling the way he imagined a flying saucer might whistle.

"Give me a break," snapped Lucas. "I'm serious here. Do you want to hear this or not?"

"Yeah, yeah," he said. "Go ahead. I'm all ears. Even though there are those who say I'm all mouth." Todd frowned. "That might be true."

Lucas rolled his eyes. "Yes, they could be right. Now listen. A few days ago, I started seeing fog in the elevator. It kinda swirled around my feet and then would disappear. It never happened when anyone else was around."

Todd held in a laugh by pretending to choke. "Thank goodness! That would definitely be something that affected tips."

Lucas, his features serious, looked steadily at his friend.

"All right, already!" said Todd. "I'm not laughin'! I'm not! A chip was caught in my throat. This is all very believable. I get fogged out every time I fly in an airplane, so why not fog in an elevator?"

"I think I'll forget telling you this," said Lucas. "Let's hit the water." Lucas got up and moved toward the warm, calm waters of the Florida gulf coast.

"Wait a minute," said Todd. "I really *am* sorry. It's just that it all seems so farfetched. I'm over goofing around now. Go on."

Lucas sat back down and remained quiet for a moment, looking at the water through confused eyes. "I may be going nuts, Todd," he said. "My mother says it's nothing, but I know better. Yesterday something happened. I knew then that I had to talk to somebody." He looked at Todd seriously. "Sorry, pal. But it looks like it's gotta be you."

Todd's early playful mood seemed to leave him. He patted Lucas on the back. "Look, ol' buddy. I know I'm a pain in the butt, but I'm always here for you. Just like Dr. Seuss. Go on with the story."

Lucas sighed. "Okay. Yesterday, I started seeing things in the elevator. Like pictures of the past. The fog swirled up and the back mirror of the elevator disappeared, and there was this other place. I could've walked right into it! Just like a time warp or something on the old *Star Trek* shows. This place, this city I saw...well it looked like this city must've looked around the turn of the century. There were Model-T Fords and horses pulling buggies and people dressed in weird clothes... Right out of the past. Really freaked me out!"

"I guess so," remarked Todd. "If elevators start acting like television sets—well, we got trouble. Does your TV set move up and down?"

"This is a big joke to you, isn't it?" Lucas was angry and a bit hurt by his friend's continual playfulness. "My life is crumbling before me, and you make jokes."

Seeing Lucas's agitation, Todd straightened up. "Sorry. Just tryin' to lighten things up. You need me as a de-stressor. Go on. Scenes in the elevator."

"Right. I saw them, off and on, all day yesterday. So, I started asking around to see if the hotel was haunted or something, and nobody knew anything."

"This is heavy duty, pal," said Todd. "But I gotta tell ya...it *does* sound crazy."

"Don't you think I know that?" Lucas buried his head in his hands for a moment and then looked up. "But I'm not stupid, Todd. Remember that fellow from the college who was at the hotel a couple days ago for a convention about medical breakthroughs. The one into hypnosis?"

"Do I!" replied Todd. "That fruit cake wanted to use me as a guinea pig in front of all those people. No way I was gone be a chicken for anybody."

Lucas smiled and shook his head. "I listened to his talk through the conference kitchen doors. It was really good, and the guy knew his stuff. He wasn't doin' any chicken stuff, Todd."

"Don't tell me you plan to go to a hypnotist?" asked Todd. "What could somebody like that tell you about all this?"

"He could tell me whether I was nuts or whether it was really happening to me. Besides, I'm not planning on going."

Todd sighed with relief.

"I *am* going. Eventually." Lucas's voice, though quiet, was firm.

"I don't believe it!" said Todd. "And to think, you'd consider going to a hypnotist without telling me!"

"I had to," Lucas admitted. "I wanted to find out whether I was crazy or what."

"Well, what did the quack say when you made this appointment to be hypnotized?" asked Todd, readjusting his swimsuit. The sand was sticking to his oiled body.

"First, I told him everything I knew over the phone. He thinks the whole thing is a past-life experience. And who does he think is a prominent figure?"

"The lady of perfection?" asked Todd.

"Yup. And get this. Later, back at the elevator, I started to see her in the foggy scenes. And she was reaching out for me to come to her." Lucas paused and looked hesitantly at his friend. "So, I did."

"You did what?" questioned Todd in confusion.

"I went to her. I took her hand and walked into another time through the mirror that wasn't there in the back of the elevator."

Todd looked at Lucas thoughtfully.

"Did you hear me?" asked Lucas. "I said I walked into another time."

"Yeah, I heard," replied Todd. "What can I say? Time sure flies when you're having fun? So how come you're here now?"

"That's where I'm confused. I was with her for days before I felt the need to come back. And when I did, I was."

"When you did, you was what?"

"I wanted to come back, and suddenly I was on my way back. But it was different coming back."

"Different...but the same?" said Todd.

Lucas grimaced. "What I mean is, that on the way back I came through this...this place. I didn't get a good look at it, but I was scared to death. There was something there. Something horrible. And Alexa was frightened, too."

"Who the hell's Alexa?" asked Todd in amazement. "We got a new character, or is this the Lady of Perfection or what?"

"No, Alexa is the girl. The one. I didn't know that 'til just this second." Lucas tilted his head in thought. "Didn't know her name 'til now. At least one of her names..."

"Was she with you in the scary place?"

"No. No, I don't think so."

"Well, how do you know she was frightened then?"

"I don't know. I just do. It was as though she was there, and she wasn't," said Lucas with a sigh.

"Uh huh!" said Todd. "There but not there. Good story. Good story. Go on."

"That's it. That's all there is. I'm going nuts. All this crazy stuff is happening to me—or not happening to me—and I'm going nuts!"

"Who knows?" said Todd. "Maybe not. What else did the shrink say about the dreams?"

"Hypnotist. He said that my dreams are remembrances from previous lives and that for some reason I can see into the past. He says that people usually see into the future, but that sometimes this kind of thing happens."

"Well, there ya go! A perfect explanation. You're psychic! And the girl is just a nice fringe benefit. I just have one question."

"What?"

"Well, you said you spent several days with this Alexa girl."

"Yes."

"And this all happened yesterday. Well, who was the guy here, running the elevator, while you were there? I mean, he looked and acted an awful lot like you. Ya know?"

The two boys sat for a moment in quiet thought.

"I just don't know," Lucas finally said. "The whole thing's a mystery to me, but I intend to find out what's going on."

"How?" asked Todd, slipping down to a more comfortable position flat on the beach towel.

Lucas shrugged in anguish. "I don't know. Maybe we could go back to the hotel and see if the elevator will take us back. The hotel's not busy this time of day. We could slip inside, close the doors, and see what happens."

Todd was skeptical, but the sun was burning his skin and he wanted to wash off the oil. Clean jeans would feel good. "Okay. Let's do it."

⌒⁓∙ᴑᴖ∙⁓⌒

Within an hour, the two boys were dressed and back in the hotel lobby.

"I think this might be stupid," remarked Todd. "And what are we going to say to Jerome when we take the elevator? It *is* his shift you know."

"He's a lazy bum, and he's not going to care," Lucas said with a shrug.

"Well, just saying you're not crazy...what if we go back into time or something and the elevator is stuck on another floor?" Todd's face showed an expression that said *Eeeks!*

"Won't happen. Things must stand still while I'm there. At least, they did that once."

"Okay," said Todd with doubt and then raised his eyes to the ceiling to talk. "Now I'm thinkin' he's an expert on elevator-time travel. Who's crazier?"

Lucas peeked into the elevator operator's cubicle. "Hey, Jerome! Todd and I are going up to the fourth for a minute, 'kay?"

"No problem," answered Jerome, without looking up from his tablet.

The elevator looked like an open maw with its doors open—not inviting at all. In fact, it seemed spooky to the boys, which was a new concept for Todd. Physical things did not often scare him—they just made him laugh to dispel the fear. The two walked inside, slowly, and turned to face outward.

"Here goes nothin'," remarked Todd.

Once the doors closed, an uncomfortable silence hung in the air around them. Even the whir of the machinery that lifted and lowered the elevator seemed distant and muted. It was though something in the air was stealing the noise of life and replacing it with the sounds of nothingness.

"I feel nervous," said Todd. "It feels creepy here. Don't recall feeling like this in an elevator before. Maybe it *is* haunted. I've heard of that kind of stuff. Why not on an elevator?"

Lucas just looked at Todd and began to take the elevator up, keeping its pace slow and steady

At that instant, fog seemed to seep out of every crack. It swirled about their legs and blinded their eyes. Todd gripped Lucas's arm.

"I told ya! Look!" cried Lucas. The mirror at the back of the elevator had disappeared and a farm scene with gentle rolling hills in the background came into view. It was like looking into a painting. Lucas took Todd's arm and pulled him forward and into the scene. When they looked back, the elevator was gone.

"Now we've done it," whispered Todd, gloom in his voice. A huge red barn was right in front of them now, and Todd fell to his knees beside the building frame and pounded on the wood. "It's real, Lucas. No dream. No fantasy. Solid."

"I know," whispered Lucas. "I told you."

Todd struggled to stand up and turned to Lucas. Swallowing hard, he attempted to keep his thoughts light. "This is not our back yard, however." His voice was full of fear and he was no longer cracking jokes.

"No kidding." Lucas continued to look around without moving.

"What is happening here?" Todd said in a whisper. He turned in a full circle.

"Ya see? It's just like I told you. We're just...here."

"Where, Lucas? Where?"

"I don't know. That's the problem. In the past, I think. Do you recognize anything?" he asked Todd, who was still actively looking around him in bewilderment, his panic growing by the second.

"Are you kidding me?" answered Todd. "No. I don't recognize anything!" He stopped, holding his hands up in the air. "Okay. Good story. Good trick. Let's go back now."

"I don't know how, Todd. I don't even know how we got here. The last time, Alexa pulled me through! We just walked into it this time."

"Great. Just great. Come on now, Lucas. I gotta be home for dinner in just half an hour and if I'm late, I'll miss my mother's best recipe: Kentucky Fried Chicken from the drive-through. Now quit playing around here."

"I'm not playing around, I tell ya. This is the stuff I've been going through, Todd. Do you understand why I'm so nuts?"

"Yeah! But who knew it was contagious? What are we gonna do?" whined Todd.

"Hey Toad!" a female voice cried out, interrupting their conference. "Toad, where are you?"

Todd looked at Lucas with disbelief. "Lucas, am I hearing things or was that Barbara? That could not be Barbara from math class. That would mean she was time traveling, too."

"Sounded like her to me," whispered Lucas.

A young girl appeared from around the side of the barn.

"There you are, Toad!" she giggled. She was dressed in a pale peasant dress and had fresh flowers in her blonde hair.

Todd and Lucas looked behind them, unsure as to whom the girl was speaking.

"Am I hearing and seeing things?" whispered Todd from the corner of his mouth. "Did Barbara—standing there in flesh and blood, dressed like a peasant or something—call me...*Toad*? People are calling me *Toad*? Oh, this cannot get any stranger. Plus, that's a demeaning name. Not that I don't like frogs and such..." He wrinkled his nose in disgust at the image.

"Sure sounds like her to me," answered Lucas quietly, and then added, "Toad."

"Everybody's a comedian," mumbled Todd. "Now who needs to stop?"

"I've been looking everywhere for you, honey," cooed the young girl to Todd and she moved close to him.

Todd glanced at Lucas with a look that said, "I don't believe this is happening."

"Barbara," began Todd, grabbing hold of Lucas's arm and pulling him toward the barn, "would you excuse us for just one short moment?"

"Barbara?" she snapped. "My name is Carmella! How could you forget that? Who is this 'Barbara'?"

"What? Oh! Carmella! Yes! Carmella!" stuttered Todd. "I...I was just thinking of my dear long, lost...cousin...Barbara."

Lucas watched the two with a stunned amusement when Todd pulled him into the barn.

"Look," he said to Lucas, "I don't care what you do, but don't take us back yet! I've been wanting to get Barbara to like me for two years!" Then he began to wring his hands, "I can't believe I said that."

"That's not Barbara, Todd," said Lucas.

"She sure looks like Barbara to me."

"She is, but she isn't," said Lucas. "She's Carmella. Remember, she said her name was Carmella?"

"Look, pal. Whether she is or she isn't or she does or she doesn't, I'm just tellin' you that I might wanna stay in the matrix for a little while longer to understand this a little better. So, don't go wishin' or thinking for your elevator or something stupid like that."

"Wishing. Thinking. Yeah. You're right. That's the key. Wishing or thinking. That's how we got here and how I got back before. I just thought it, and it was."

"Not now, Lucas!" said Todd, moving to the door. "Please! I'm not scared anymore! We need to do some research on this! You know I'm right!"

The barn door opened and both boys' mouths fell open. Another girl stood in front of them.

"Lucas," she said, moving to stand in front of him. "You've come back."

"Alexa," was all Lucas could whisper.

"You're right," muttered Todd. "She's beautiful."

Alexa turned to Todd for the first time, the softness of her white cotton morning dress hanging in folds about her. "You are welcome here," she said to him, "but will you stay?"

"Toad!" called Carmella from outside the barn. "Are you coming?"

Todd said, "Thank you for the kind welcome, and I will stay for a while." He paused and glanced at Lucas. "Won't I, Lucas? Will we be investigators?"

"I don't know," said Lucas softly. "I don't feel right being here. I don't understand any of this."

Alexa's eyes grew big and tears began to traipse down to her cheeks. "Don't go, Lucas!" She sniffed. "Don't leave me again!"

Then the two boys were no longer in the barn but floating down a long dark hallway toward a black pit. Fear held them quiet, their eyes wide with faltering anticipation. They clung to each other.

"I don't like this!" yelled Todd over a continuous sound of...noise. It sounded almost like machinery but was coarse and offensive to the ears like nails on a chalkboard. "You just had to wish us away didn't you?"

"I'm sorry!" said Lucas. "I just couldn't stay! And I don't know how I did it. And I didn't wish for this place, whatever it is...It's dangerous. I know that for sure."

"No kidding," yelled Todd.

A roar could be heard from the pit over top the monotonous noise and a voice from behind them. Alexa's voice. "No!" she screamed. "They shall pass!"

Lucas and Todd suddenly were no longer in the Black Place but sat on the floor of the elevator staring at each other, the past only a shadow of insanity now.

Todd pulled a piece of chewing gum from his pocket and crammed it into his mouth. "Wow, Lucas. When you dream, you don't fool around. I really wanted to stay with Barbara though, ya know?"

"It wasn't—"

"I know," he interrupted. "I know it wasn't her. So, what happened to us, anyway? Are we both nuts now? Guilt by association or something like that?"

"I think I need to talk to that hypnotist," said Lucas softly. "This is no longer just me being psychic. It's physical, and you're in it, too. There's more to this whole thing. I just know there is."

"Yeah," agree Todd. "That roar from that pit place was not somebody's hunger pangs; that's for sure. At least I hope not. I really didn't like that part, kiddo."

The boys looked at each other with raised eyebrows.

"Will you go with me to the hypnotist, Todd," Lucas asked. "I'm a little edgy about this."

"Sure, couldn't keep me away."

"Thanks," said Lucas. "There's just one thing I have to do first. You go on home and I'll meet you back here in an hour or so."

Todd nodded with concern. "You just take it easy, pal. New friends are too hard to break in. And stay away from elevators."

"I hear you," said Lucas, his thoughts elsewhere as he took the elevator down.

3

PEOPLE OF THE HILL

"*Djiionondo wanenaka!*" whispered Lucas hoarsely, his breath coming in short pants.

"English, Lucas," interrupted the doctor. "Everything you see, hear, and say will be translated into English. Do you understand?"

Lucas, his muscles a bit strained in the overstuffed recliner, stretched and then merely nodded.

"Just let it all pour out as it happens—your feelings, your observations...And relax. Go ahead now, Lucas. Tell me what is happening." The young doctor pulled nervously at his mustache.

"People of the Moving Time," began Lucas again in a soft voice. A drop of sweat shone on his brow.

Lucas could not hear the doctor, nor remember the cool leather of the chair beneath him. He was no longer in the present, but in the distant past— the seventeenth century.

Dressed in trappers' clothing, dirty and blood-streaked, Lucas struggled with the ropes that bound his wrists together, and he cursed the terrible accident that had left the man dead.

The Moving Time tribe was known for fierce behavior. More than just difficult to deal with, they were cause for fear. Despite the bloodthirsty men Lucas had come to know since his arrival in the Northeastern part of the wilderness country, he still could dig deep into his own soul and feel the fear of death that the others did not think about.

He stumbled in silence behind the black stallion, ridden by an angry warrior, who glared frequently over his shoulder at Lucas. A long rope pulled hard at the cords binding his wrists, and Lucas struggled to keep enough slack to prevent the jolting pain that tore up his arms.

Shuddering, he walked on. Minutes faded into what seemed hours before Lucas could see the high fence surrounding the village, protecting their camp from surprise attacks. The settlement was situated at the fork of the great river where cool waters flowed into a natural lake.

Through the sweat dripping from Lucas's forehead and into his eyes, he could see the children—some not much younger than him—romping just beyond the tall barriers. The scene was a pleasant one and, for a moment, a feeling of relief swept over him. In such a place where children played so innocently, there could be no danger. Could there?

The warrior jerked on the rope, sending spasms of pain to Lucas's wrists and arms yet again. Holding in a groan of agony, he swallowed hard, licked his cracked lips, and forgot the feeling of relief. He was marching to his death.

Moving through the opening in the fence, Lucas caught his first glimpse of the famous longhouses that his trapper companions often spoke of. Though he hunted with the others, he had never witnessed this way of life.

As the warrior spoke in his own tongue to a woman just inside the entranceway, Lucas looked about him with fearful interest. Any thought helped him forget the pain in his arms. There seemed to be six longhouses in the village, all sitting side by side. The structures were rectangular and measured anywhere from two to three times as long as wide. The high roof of each house was arched, giving an open-air effect. Thin lines of smoke curled lazily up through the rooves of the windowless longhouses at equal distances from each other.

"Cozy," thought Lucas just before the warrior on the horse jerked hard on the rope, knocking him to the ground. The rider allowed the horse to dart forward dragging Lucas along behind. It took some distance for him to gather enough strength to pull himself up to a standing position to run behind the horse—a sloppy and painful effort at best. An earlier gash on Lucas's face was again opened from his fall to the ground, and his skin stung from the salted tears streaming unbidden down his face. Trying to control his emotions, he took in his breath and held it, trotting behind the horse that led him throughout the busy village for all to see.

Men, women, and children stopped their work and play to look at the man who had again begun the blood feud between the races. Their faces were blank, and Lucas turned his eyes away in a shame that was not really his to feel. Although it was true that he was not guilty of the crime he would be punished for, he knew that this culture stated that someone must pay for crimes against the tribe. The whole incident had been a terrible accident—one that Lucas could not have helped. But now he would pay—despite the circumstances. Blood repaid blood. The People of the Moving Time saw it no other way.

Finally, after suffering the humiliating and frightening trot through the village, the warrior came to stop before the longhouse furthermost from the main opening in the barricaded fence. Lucas looked up, weary, wondering what new act of punishment would be thrown at him.

Above the longhouse door, a picture of a wolf—it's teeth sharp and pointed—was painted. He looked around to another longhouse doorway and saw a turtle. Lucas gulped, thinking that a wolf was much more cunning and dangerous than a turtle.

The warrior jumped down from his horse and, with the assistance of two others, tied Lucas to a stake near the doorway of the wolf longhouse.

"Anuska!" cried out the warrior, making Lucas jump from the sudden boom of his voice.

A woman appeared from the longhouse and to the warrior, who answered her, bowed and left, moving the crowd of onlookers aside as he went.

Lucas studied the woman with wide eyes; he was afraid, yet drawn by her appearance.

She stood before him, black eyes sparking and hair so dark that purple highlights seemed to spring from the braids at either side of her head. Her skin, darkly tanned from the sun's rays, looked soft and delicate, despite the obvious strength shown in her lightly muscled body. This one was definitely not delicate. She was dressed differently than the other women of the village, the line of her animal skin dress cut more harshly and a beaded belt was tied around her waist. The dress hung about her in a tattered fashion, moving with the wind's gentle breeze. Her feet were bare.

Lucas stared at her.

She stood silently waiting for him to acknowledge her.

He finally let his eyes fall. This woman held his life in her hands. He swallowed hard before looking back to her face.

"Well," she said, her voice flowing through her lips like cream. "Is your name as it has always been?"

Lucas stared a moment into her eyes, before he realized that he had understood the woman's words. "You speak my language?" he asked in quiet amazement.

"I speak *your* language," she replied simply, obviously amused by his puzzled stare.

"Look," he began, peering around him like the trapped animal he was, "I had nothing to do with your husband's death. I'm sorry, though. Really! I...I, it was an accident! You must believe me! Please!" He stopped, seeing that his begging made her uncomfortable, and he bit down hard on his lower lip, waiting for her to speak.

She moved around him, looking at him closely. For the first time in his life, Lucas felt self-conscious. His skin, though white, was tanned, and his wide, powerful shoulders and chest showed how hard he worked for his living. Through torn trousers, taut legs caked with dried blood held his body against the stake.

She smiled and then looked directly into his eyes.

Frowning, Lucas looked at the woman more closely and tilted his head in question. He had seen her before. He was sure of it. But where? Was that even possible?

She smiled again. "Yes, dear one. You remember something?"

"Yes," he replied, and then added, "no. No."

"I thought not."

"What will you do with me?" He couldn't quell the tremor to his voice.

"It is my right to sentence you to death." She waited for response from him.

Lucas held his panic in check and did not change expression. This woman was trying to manipulate him. She was amused by his fear. He promised himself that he would not show his vulnerable side again—though it might mean his own death.

She smiled and nodded, pleased with his control. "Or," she began again, "I could see you tortured."

Again, Lucas remained silent.

"Which would you like?" she asked, moving her face closer to his.

Feeling her breath on his cheek, he answered, "Neither."

"I could see you spared," she said teasingly, "if you can show me something about you worth sparing. It is my choice. I can see you die for what you did to my husband, or—should you prove yourself a good provider to me—and to my tribe—I could adopt you as my new husband."

She walked slowly around him, and then tilted his head roughly down to her face. "Of course, if I were to take you as my husband and you fell back to your old ways, or if you failed to please me in the manner to which I am accustomed, I could banish you or have you killed at any time. It is my right."

Lucas's mind swirled. His choices were very limited, but there was a glimmer of hope hidden deep within those options. It seemed his choice was either death by torture or taking a Seneca wife. He did not want to die, but, at the same time, he felt he was not old enough to marry. Sixteen was too young for his liking—though many did that very thing these days—and he knew very little about marriage. But she was beautiful—perhaps the most beautiful girl he had ever seen. He smiled thinly.

"I see you have chosen," she remarked, her expression smug.

"How is it that you speak my language so well?" He tried to change the subject so that what was coming to him would not come. He could not think clearly now and was frightened by the decision he had been forced to make to save his life.

"I have been waiting for you. I always speak your language. You do not understand now. But you will understand one day. Possibly. For now, it would suit you to learn the ways of the People, for this is my home in this life. And now, it is yours."

"I don't understand. What do you mean? Please tell me."

"I cannot. I will not. But you must obey. You will obey. You will run the gauntlet," she instructed.

"The gauntlet?" he questioned, not understanding her meaning.

"The challenge of combat."

"I have to fight?" he exclaimed. "And then what? If I win, do I get my freedom?"

"In a sense," she said. "But you will not fight for your freedom."

"Then what?"

"This is my home," she said, waving her arm to the longhouse with the likeness of the wolf over the doorway. "We in this house are the Clan of the Wolf. You must run through the village and suffer the beatings of all the women and children in the tribe as you try to reach this house. They will use clubs and whips. If you falter or fall, you will be tied to the stake and called a weakling, and you will be killed as such. If you are successful, you will be free the moment you reach the door of the Clan of the Wolf. My clan. Free to be my husband and brother in the tribe. That is the extent of your freedom. The women rule the home in this time and place. Should I tire of you, or should you attempt an escape, I would see you die. It is my right." She looked about her for a few seconds and then whispered, "You should try not to do that—escape that is. It would set things back..."

Lucas studied her face and managed to hold in a smile. She would not see him killed. This was evident in her face and her manner. She, for some reason beyond his understanding, was drawn to him. He would, at first chance, escape into the nearby wooded area and make his way back to the trading post before he was even missed by this woman. He would not heed her warning, because she knew nothing of his strength and willingness to do what it took to get away.

He would take this challenge of combat and would not fall, and then he would pretend to become her husband. But, looking back at her face, Lucas hesitated in thought. She was not a woman to take lightly. He shivered; he felt that she could see into his soul, know his thoughts, and control his desires. Looking closely at her now, he could see that she was smiling at him, taunting him, amused with his hidden plans.

"When do I run this gauntlet?" he asked, trying to tear her probing eyes from his mind.

"As soon as you are prepared," she answered. "You are injured. Do you wish to have your wounds dressed first?"

"No," replied Lucas, not wanting her to think him weak. "These are mainly just scratches. Just cut me down from this post."

She nodded and called out for a warrior's assistance. After speaking to the warrior for a moment, she paused and spoke to Lucas. "All will be made ready. You will stay with my brother here until the time is right."

"Wait!" said Lucas, before she disappeared into the longhouse. "Your name. Who will I be running for?"

She smiled and threw back her head in a teasing fashion. "Anuska. My name is Anuska."

"Do you want to know mine?" he asked her.

"No," she replied. "You will be mine to name, should you survive." With that, she turned and moved into the longhouse.

The warrior at Lucas's side displayed no emotion as he slit the ropes holding Lucas to the stake. His body finally free, Lucas rubbed his tender wrists and massaged his arms. The warrior stood silent, facing him.

"Relax, friend," said Lucas under his breath. "The lady likes me."

Only a short time passed before a group of women left Anuska's longhouse, led by an elderly female with the face of death itself (or so it seemed). Lucas, who now sat in front of the guarding warrior, rose to his feet, aware that something serious was about to take place.

The old woman made angry hand signals in his direction and growled some sort of ritual song. It was not a good sound.

Lucas raised his eyebrows in question and gritted his teeth into a false smile as he looked to Anuska for explanation.

Her face was hard and gone was the romantic lure she had thrown his way earlier. Somehow, he felt less sure of himself with all the cold stares. Clubs and whips really could be brutal, even if the blows were coming from women and children. He briefly wondered when the young boys of this tribe were considered men.

"The time has come," she said and turned to the other women. A moment later, turning back to Lucas. "I have spoken of my husband's death, caused by you, to my sisters of the Clan. They feel my loss, my pain, my need. But they pity me.

Because you are not of this time. Not of our kind and, therefore, not of our spirit. The Gods may be harsh with our house, and they fear your entrance as my husband, should you survive the gauntlet. But it is my choice, and I have made my decision. Take care, for this is a violent test of strength, and I can offer you no assistance. But rest assured, once you have reached my house and have entered, no matter your state of mind and body, you will be a brother to the tribe. Accepted as one of us—for as long as you *are* one of us. I will prepare for you, while you struggle. May the Gods bring you to me."

"Anuska!" Lucas called out to her.

She turned toward him, her features again warm.

"I will survive this test," he informed her. "And I will not disappoint you."

She smiled and replied, "I know. You never do." Turning away from him, she entered the longhouse followed by the other women in her Clan. He was alone, again, with the warrior guard.

Frowning, he looked past the guard, trying to see into the dark interior of the longhouse. What had Anuska meant? "You never do," she had said.

Another twinge of familiarity overwhelmed him. Where did he know her from? She was certainly not like the other women he had seen this day. She was educated and well-spoken in the languages of others. *His* language was among that. And when she looked at him...it was as though she could see into his very mind and soul. His every whim and need surfaced in her dark, knowing eyes.

Who was this girl, and why did he feel so strongly about her? It was certainly not the right time for such feelings to take over. He was in real trouble here.

Lucas sighed hard and jumped, startled when the warrior grabbed his arm to pull him away from the longhouse of the Wolf Clan.

4

THE GAUNTLET

Lucas stood proudly at the far end of the village, ready to run the gauntlet for his freedom. Looking down at his hands, he saw—and felt—that they were still bleeding from the rope burns at being dragged by the horse. There was pain, and he winced, gingerly touching his fingers. His muscles ached and his stomach felt as though he'd been recently punched. Of course, that was exactly what had happened.

"What have I gotten myself into?" he whispered to himself. "I'm not going to make it out of here alive."

He could see rows of women and children lining the way to Anuska's longhouse, all armed with heavy clubs and whips. These were the same children playing in the fields the day before, the same women cooking over open fires to feed their families. Now they were terrifying to him because they represented what might be his death.

Lucas had lost all confidence in his ability to make it through this trial of torture.

Behind him, two warriors stood armed with newly acquired rifles that the French brought to the native population. Who knew that a business he'd become so familiar with would be part of his undoing? How often had he been close enough to hear the traders swap their wares—guns being just one of the sought-after treasures.

A war cry sounded from the far end of the village, and a warrior behind Lucas nudged him hard with the butt of a rifle. The time had come.

Lucas sucked in his breath and willed himself to gather some appearance of courage. This was something he had to do. If not, he would submit to the tragic will of death. A tear threatened to roll down his cheek, but he quickly brushed it away. The sting of that salted tear burned when it touched his wounded hand, but he made his mind ignore it.

Earlier, Lucas had stood tall and straight. Now, he slouched a bit, hopeless at the thought of what was ahead. Anuska had said that he must prove himself to her. He sighed, afraid of what he would have to face to do that. But no; he knew what he had to face. It was clear and right in front of him. There was murder in the eyes of the women and children who would hound him with their weapons.

He took a deep breath and ran.

The agony of the first strikes did not reach his mind at first. He was aware only of masses of color from the attackers all blurring together as he streaked through the village. The far-off forest, green and tempting, called him to the cool streams, and distant birds whispered his name as though they knew him, beckoning him to their safe haven of wood. But the fantasy was distorted by colorful beads and the deepness of foreign eyes. Fighting the blows to his body, Lucas dodged the pounding clubs and cracking whips hitting and biting his flesh. He ran as hard as he could.

The longhouse could be reached by passing through any number of passages between the buildings, but those ways were always blocked by harassing children, their ammunition bruising his skin and pushing surges of pain to his mind as they struck him. They were laughing and enjoying their insanity. It mattered not that he was a living, breathing being. They only did what they were urged to do by their elders. And the elders wanted him dead.

The dusty ground was stained red, and his eyes were blinded with his own blood. The fear of failure choked him. But something deep inside carried him on—blow after blow, slash after slash. Anuska would have a new husband. And she would pay for this humiliation. He would see to it. He would not forget this treachery. He would remember it until he was well into his next life.

Lucas blinked for a second, still running as fast as his body would allow. Next life? What had he been thinking? In that instant, it was as though time stopped around him and madness took over. The women and children, coarse and screaming, were only visions without motion. Their mouths were open to taunt him but no sound came out. No movement carried them forward. They were still, just as he seemed to be, in motion but stopped in space. He was somewhere else, some other land, some other time. And she was there—this Anuska...and he loved her.

But with an unexpected slam of a club to his thigh, he was back in the present, everything moving, and he'd forgotten the connection. All he could see now was the cruelty ahead. Anger propelled him forward, though his pace slowed as the blows became more frequent and hardier. The stronger women and children seemed to be situated on the last leg of the run, or possibly he was just too beaten to notice there was no real difference.

A war club made painful contact to his midsection, stopping Lucas in his tracks, and he bent over, clutching his stomach. The man inside Lucas wanted to strike out at the young boy who had delivered such a crippling blow, but through the blood he saw that he could not do this. At a distance, a rifle was aimed at him, ready to fire, should he attack his attacker.

Lucas cringed in agony, but straightened a bit when he saw, through wet eyes, that the longhouse of the Wolf was not more than fifty feet from him. Just a short dash. A few more assaults and he would be free.

Free to belong to the tribe.

He sucked in his last remaining breath, pulling courage from the deepest part of his soul...and ran.

The final attacks to his body were brutal and his last conscious thought before dropping to the soft earth floor inside the longhouse was that, even now, because of all his wounds, he might not survive.

Then all went black.

The light was dim when Lucas awoke, his temples aching and his body weak from the run. He wasn't sure he wasn't dead. The end had been bad, and he'd welcomed death. But he wasn't dead. He could tell, and he needed to have a plan.

Lucas lay very still, leaving his eyes open only enough to look over his surroundings, but not enough for anyone to know he was now conscious. He played "opossum."

In the dark, cozy interior of the longhouse, many small fires along a narrow central walkway spread dancing firelight throughout the windowless home of the Clan of the Wolf. Smells of soot, sweat, kettle soup, and tobacco filled his nose, and the smoke, although drawn through the ceiling vents, stung his eyes, making them water. Feeling the need to wipe the smoke from his eyes, he wrinkled his nose and squinted.

From out of nowhere, it seemed, a cool, damp cloth came down across his forehead and gentle hands cleansed his face and eyes.

"Awake, I see," said Anuska softly.

"Yes," he replied, trying to rise, but falling back in exhaustion.

"I knew. But I wished not to disturb you. The smoke in your eyes led my hands to you." With that, she dipped the cloth back into a nearby container of water, rinsed it, and then began to wash away the sweat and dried blood from his face.

Lucas fought hard to stay calm. Gazing around him, he was surprised at the warm, homey scene. There were many families living together in the longhouse, and it seemed that at least two families shared each of the six fires along the long walkway. Each family "apartment" could be curtained off for privacy by animal skins hung from the rafters or frames woven with cornhusks. Platform beds of bearskin and seats made from bark and logs were situated along both sides of the long walls beneath lengthy, wooden shelves storing household belongings—pots and kettles, foods, and weapons. Braids of corn, strings of dried squash and apples, and hanks of tobacco hung on the walls or from the rafters.

A white lizard stood watching him from a nearby shelf. Lucas grimaced slightly.

This was crazy. This whole practice of taking someone and just making them a husband to a woman he didn't even know or care for was insane. How did these people expect him to adjust to their way of life? To become one of them? Surely this was not the rule for treatment of prisoners. Why had Anuska wanted him so badly? How could he measure up to her standards of a Seneca man, to her husband now gone, when he was no more than a boy and knew virtually nothing of her way of life? Nor did he want to.

Anuska brushed the lizard away and placed her arms around Lucas.

❧

"Where am I?" said Lucas, rubbing his eyes.

"What do you mean, 'Where am I?'" cried Todd. "What happened next?"

"Remain calm, boys," said the doctor. "I think this session is over."

"Over!" said Todd. "He was getting to the best part! How can it be over now?"

"Wait a minute," interrupted Lucas. "What happened? Was I under?"

"Under!" cried Todd. "You were so far under, you could've dug out in China!"

"Lucas," said the doctor, waving his hand to quiet Todd. "Yes, you were under, and I took you back to another life in the seventeenth century.

And yes, to agree with your friend, the whole experience was very interesting. But you came out all by yourself. I had nothing to do with it. Apparently, something inside you did not want to share the rest of this particular story with us. Listen, and please don't think me rude if I take more notes."

The doctor allowed the tape player to retell the story for Lucas.

"Wow," Lucas whispered. "What does all this mean? How does it fit?"

"We don't really know," replied the doctor, looking up from his notebook. "Past-life regression is not fully understood or believed these days. In fact, most in my field think it is nothing more than either daydreaming or that the hypnotist places these suggestions into their patients. We don't know where all this comes from—only that it seems to be quite real for some. And, of course, there are those who disbelieve past-life regression all together—religious or scientific reasons and such. They won't even discuss it. And I'm afraid that I cannot explain the scenes from the elevator, either. This is the very first time I've heard of an actual case where someone could step physically into another time. Even I am having difficulty believing it all. I do think, however, that something more powerful is at work here than the mere past-life occurrence I initially thought."

"Like what?" asked Todd.

"I really don't know, young man," answered the doctor. "I wish I could help you. I, of course, find the case very interesting and would be happy to hypnotize you again, but I don't know how that will help these things happening at your hotel.

"And, you know, this may not even be past life at all, as I mentioned. Maybe there really is another world or parallel lives. Very unscientific of me to say that, but...I really don't know."

⌘

"I don't know," said Todd, frowning, his voice showing signs of discomfort.

"We have to! I mean, if we want to find out what's going on, we've got to take a chance or two," said Lucas, cutting into the restaurant's dinner special of the day. "You didn't have a hand in cooking this, did you?"

"Nah," answered Todd. "I'm just scrapping plates this summer."

Lucas continued as he ate, "Anyway, how come you're scared all of a sudden? Before, when we tried it, you wanted to stay." Then he added, "I know one thing, I'm starving. Ever since that hypnosis session, I can't get enough food. Anyway, like I asked, why so scared now?"

"I know; I know I seem scared and before I wasn't, but my hormones were stirred up. I've had some time to think now, though. That hypnotist scared the bagongas out of me. I think you could easily step off that elevator and into the same territory you talked about while you were under. And personally, Lucas old pal, I don't care to get scalped along with you. That was one frightening roller coaster ride, that time travel stuff. Things feel just a little too real around you of late. In fact, crazy or not, things are real in that other place— the one we went into in the elevator. I felt it, too."

"That's true. Things are real, all right. But Todd, there's got to be a reason for all this. Suppose there are different lives for everyone, all happening at the same time in different places. 'Til now, I haven't been aware of any of it. Then, all of a sudden, I'm thrown smack dab into the middle of these other lives. I really don't think it's a common thing for people to walk through elevator doors into the past, do you? Something has upset the balance of time...or something."

Todd shook his head and took another bite of his supper. "My initial response would be to hum the theme from *Star Trek*, but for once, I'm so mixed up, I can't even show my wonderful disrespect. Or even choose my song, because...like...*Twilight Zone* would fit, too. And in a way, even *The Simpsons*—"

"Like you know the meaning of respect to begin with," said Lucas, interrupting and then laughing.

"You hurt me, pal!" said Todd, pretending to be shot. Then his face became serious. "I know what you're saying, though. Of course, something's not right. This shouldn't be happening. And you're involved right up to your eyeballs. Even so, I don't know if I want to go back in that elevator again. My eyeballs are...well mine. And they don't want to be involved. So, I don't think I want to go."

"Me neither, but I have to. With or without you," decided Lucas. "So, make up your mind."

"Oh, yeah. Lay the guilt on me." Todd groaned his sarcasm evident. "Okay. I'll go. I know I'm gonna be sorry, but I'll go."

Lucas and Todd stood inside the closed elevator facing what should've been the back mirrored panel.

"I don't like the looks of this," remarked Todd.

"No," said Lucas, scratching behind his ear, "I think you may be right."

Instead of the mirror, there was a wooden door with a big brass handle shaped like a biting dog. There were no inside doors in elevators. Not this kind of door or any kind of door.

Words appeared and disappeared on the door. First, ENTER AT YOUR OWN RISK, then, DO NOT ENTER, RISKY, and finally, SAVE ME.

"The *save me* message is from her," said Lucas. "I just know it."

"Yeah, right." Todd was not entirely convinced. "Save her from what? That's what worries me. Remember that roar we heard before, in that dark place we came through?"

"Ummmmm," muttered Lucas with an absent nod. "Looks like we don't have a choice, though. Have you noticed that the elevator has stopped between floors? And that cannot be good at all."

Todd moved to pull at the lever, but the elevator would not budge. "So, what do we do? Go through a door that says DO NOT ENTER? And how come this door is here, anyway? Before you said there was always a scene to walk into."

Lucas shrugged. "I don't know."

"Maybe we could just open it a crack," suggested Todd. "Then we can slam it shut if some monster breathes on us or anything."

Both boys shuffled about, both trying to come up with ideas.

"Okay," agreed Lucas finally. "That's a good idea. We'll open it just a crack to see and that's all." They got ready to move forward.

"Get ready," said Lucas. He stepped up to the door and grabbed the brass knob. "Ahhhh!" he yelled and pulled his hand away. "The handle bit me! Can you believe that? This door that's not supposed to be here bit me!"

"Great, doors that bite," whispered Todd, glancing at Lucas's hand. "No marks, though. But look," he said pointing to the knob. "Grab it now; the dog's mouth is shut!"

Without hesitation, Lucas grabbed the knob again. This time there was no bite, just a muffled sound of an animal smothering. "It must be real in some way or it wouldn't sound like that..."

"Now I've seen everything," said Todd. "A doorknob with breathing problems."

"Shut up!" ordered Lucas softly. "And get around here so you can see, too, when I open it.

Let's do this while we can or before we chicken out. Ready?"

Not waiting for his friend's reply, Lucas pulled at the door. Nothing happened. He yanked at it. Nothing happened.

"It must be locked," he said. The dog face on the handle had large, dark, mean eyes. And they were staring hard at him.

"Well, whatever you do, don't let go of the handle! The dog's mouth might open again. And that thing looks pretty agitated. Try one more time," said Todd.

Just as Lucas began to turn the knob and pull again, the message on the door changed: PUSH.

The boys looked at each other, fearful. This was truly bizarre.

"The door knows we're going to look inside," whispered Todd.

"Listen to you," said Lucas. "Doors can't know anything."

"True," agreed Todd. "And elevators can't take people on vacations either, but this one does."

"Okay, point made," Lucas said, dismissing his rational thoughts. "I'm going to push now. I'm going on record to say that this is probably not a good idea, but hey...whatever."

5

THE BLACK PLACE

The Monster waited in the Black Place. It watched. It moved back and forth. It turned and twisted. The time was coming, and it was happy.

Of course, happiness was not something it could really feel, but the hatred was more powerful at these times, and that was almost the same as happiness. It had once been told that once by those in the bowels of this place. The curse would surely end this time. Victory was close.

It took time to remember the days of its old pleasure. She had been beautiful then—in the beginning, when it had been human. (It swirled in the Black Place, thinking about that...had it ever really been human or had that been a trick of the dark and the light?) The girl's name had been Anitra in that place and in that time. And she had been promised to him. It was family law. This was the way of marriage in families of magic. She was light magic and he was dark magic and they had smiled on the union.

Because of the marriage between dark and light, his ancestors would lose a portion of their evil and hers would gain a bit of that same evil. But her evil gain would not tarnish the good in her family. His gain with the union, however, would save the new generations of evil to come, and the tiny bit of acceptance of her good was merely a sneeze in the face of his dark progress. They would stay alive with the girl's help. There was hope. Without the light magic Anitra would offer him, the Creator meant to banish him and all his family to the Black Place for all time for the safe keeping of humanity. The Creator had tired of a family made of total evil, and so the marriage was arranged to see if something could be done to temper it.

Anitra, his intended, had been afraid of him, though. Though unfortunate, it made little difference in the scheme of things. She would save his family. And in return, he would show her that he was capable of great kindness—in his own way.

Even now, he smiled at that. If what he'd become could smile. It was really just the thought of a smile. As far as the kindness he'd promised, there was no true concept of meaning of that for it.

Of course, as a means of respect, he would cover the ugly face his kind was born with using magic. Dark magic was not without a price, though.

Powerful, yes.

Satisfying, yes.

But the price was beauty. He was quite ugly in human form, the worst in the family.

The monster of this current time fidgeted in its place, anger now swirling through its...body. It remembered the time when things went wrong. That boy had found his way to the castle. Son of an outland Duke, he had said. And not even part of the magic families. Anitra was young and the boy was handsome. She'd left the castle—left *him*—and went with the boy.

The Dark Family had been furious, but the Light Clan had allowed their daughter to follow her heart.

The Creator, too, had been angry. It did not matter that the dark magic family was willing and wanting to honor the bargain of marriage. The family of evil was banished from the world, from and for all time, to live as monsters in the Black

Place. They were to be a constant reminder to all evil people that the penalty for sin was great, for at the time of death, each human guilty of evil passed through the Black Place.

All people held some evil.

Each learned the terrible lesson of evil before moving on to a new life. Each passed by the monstrous dark magic monsters. Everyone passed through the Black Place without exception.

And so, it and its family had been trapped for eternity, with only a glimmer of hope for escape. The girl was still the key. If she were to open her light magic to him, even now, in the Black Place, the family would, again, be free to roam the world. She could still save them.

But she was stubborn. She hated all that his family stood for. There was no place for even a little evil in her life. The monster spun in circles, angry and frustrated.

Now, after years and years of watching and waiting, things were beginning to change. The monster took life energy from the evil of the others who passed through, giving it little shreds of strength, making it bolder and angrier. The monster had become smarter, too.

It watched the girl's lives and found that each was nearly the same. The difference was only in time and location.

Yes, yes, there were scenes and characters to play, but Anitra played with time so that she could be happy forever. Somehow, she was able to manipulate it, mold it into love, each time. The boy she'd run away with on that shameful wedding day *then* came to her in each life. She would meet him, marry him, and live a charmed life, again and again.

The goodness of her light magic spread through each generation of human nature in this way. This made all good humans lighter, brighter, and full of love...all that the Creator wanted from them.

But now, things were different. It smirked in its own way. The monster had found a tiny crack in the Black Place. Of course, there was still much evil in the world—and more each passing day, as humans were too stupid to see the manipulations of their flimsy souls. Slowly, over thousands of years, the evil in the world was slicing through to the Black Place, opening it to set the monster free.

Little by little.

Someone with hatred for another would die and pass through the Black Place, leaving a small piece of hate to be sucked in. Then another. And Another.

Wars were the best for this sucking of hate. There were times when the monster had floated through thousands of souls, gasping at the power flowing in. But even the minor evils were important at this time of the monster's being: revenge, jealousy, abuse, savagery of all kinds, no matter how small.

In a million more years—or less—it would be free *without* Anitra's hand in marriage. Free to spread real evil. Free to live again despite what the Creator said. It would be all powerful.

That was not good enough, however. The monster was tired of waiting. It wanted to seek revenge on the innocent Anitra now—in this place and in this time. It wanted to live and be human *now!*

And the sniveling boy gave it the opportunity. Not yet with her in this lifetime, the boy wasted away in a small box that moved people about a building. A strange thing...an elevator it was called...but a good thing, for it was intimate and closed in. It was just the right place to trap an innocent.

And the boy's curiosity was strong. That would be the boy's downfall—that curiosity, that self-reliable know-it-all attitude. The boy would set the monster free. The monster would be human again!

It had been easy, really. Letting pictures of previous lives slip through the crack from the Black Place to the elevator; it invited the boy to step through to another time. This was against the rules of the Creator, but the monster did not care. It knew that the boy would have to return to his own life, and when he did, he would travel through the Black Place. Not for his sin, but because the entrance to the world back to the elevator was through the tiny crack—the crack in the Black Place. The elevator was the boy's door to another time and place and he could be easily lured.

The monster floated in hatred but felt its own kind of bliss. It would capture the boy, and Anitra would follow to save him. Both the boy and its old love would be in the Black Place. The boy would be eaten without mercy! How tasty that would be.

And the girl would watch and know that she could not double-cross the evil family again. Anitra would belong to it. The monster would be free.

Then the monster had an idea. Why send the boy to another life? Why not just invite the boy to the Black Place? The boy had the taste of travel and wanted more. Why not fool him into opening the door into the Black Place? The curse could be ended once and for all! Anitra would surely come then! To save the boy! To free the evil! But it would all be for nothing.

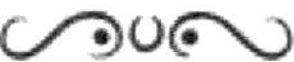

The monster floated just beyond the door in the elevator. Thrills seeped through it when the brass dog handle bit into the flesh of the boy. There was no blood in the dark world, but the boy would feel the pain of the bite when he entered the Black Place.

Oh yes! That pain and a million more!

It waited, but grew irritated with the plan.

The boys were stupid. They pulled on the door to open it instead of pushing it. The monster had to send another sign. Sending signs was dangerous. This was a very tricky plan and was not without problems. Anitra might at any time feel the monster's evil. She could stop this. And it was sure that she would. This would cause great damage to its plan.

After a moment of thought, it decided to take the chance anyway. It sent the gentle message PUSH to the door, hoping that the message SAVE ME had convinced the boy to enter beyond all thoughts of risk. Just a crack and it could suck the boy through, eat his brains!

The monster waited.

Lucas pushed the door ever so lightly, holding tight to the brass dog knob.

The door began to pull away from him, as if someone—or something—was pulling from the other side. There was a strong suction coming from the open crack of the door, swirling and pulling the air from inside the elevator into and beyond the doorway.

"Close it!" yelled Todd. "Quick! Something's sucking us in!"

"I'm trying! It's too hard!" Lucas struggled to pull the door closed but lost the battle. The door was opening, inch by inch, a black empty void pulling the boys forward. "Hold onto me!" yelled Lucas. "It's pulling me in!"

Todd threw his arms around Lucas's waist and held on. Looking around for something to catch his foot on to brace the pull, Todd looked over Lucas's shoulder into the black void behind the door.

"Ahhhhh!" he cried out. "Did you see it? Did you see that thing?"

"Yes," wheezed Lucas, his arms weakening from the pull of the door. "Whatever it is, it's alive and it wants us! We can't let it get us!"

"All I saw was a flash of teeth and eyes of fire! Right out of a horror flick!"

The boys were using all their strength now to hold the door, now open more than two inches.

"It's gonna have us soon," yelled Lucas. "Think of something!"

"I can't!" yelled Todd. "This was your idea!"

"What's happening now?" screamed Lucas. The elevator was filling with a film of rolling fog. The cold damp smell that filled the small space when the door opened was being covered by a flower-like scent. A scene was emerging to one side of the door!

"Look!" yelled Todd. "A scene!"

A moment later, the girl stood inside the elevator. *The girl.*

"Be gone!" She screamed into the blackness beyond the door.

A blood-curdling roar responded, loud enough to hurt Lucas and Todd's ears. And the monster's evil face flashed into view! It hurtled itself toward the opening door, as the boys held their ground. A horrible head squished through!

The girl leaned forward and, placing her hands over Lucas's, began to pull the door shut. But the monster was strong.

Pointed, dripping fangs latched onto the side of the door and pulled against her. She faltered and fell back, pushing Lucas to the floor in all the confusion.

The door flew open wide and the black void sucked the boys closer to the monster's gaping mouth. The gurgling noise from its throat brought goosebumps to Lucas's body as he slid toward the door.

Todd was pulling at one arm and the girl at the other, trying to slow the drag of the black void.

The girl was frightened. Her eyes were wide when she yelled, "When I say now, jump into the picture! It cannot follow us there! We'll be safe for a time!"

The boys, rapidly losing faith in their own strength, just nodded. Their fear surpassed the girl's.

"JUMP!" she yelled to them.

All three leaped toward the scene. The girl was the first through, still hanging onto Lucas's arm. She pulled and he followed her out of the elevator.

Todd was still hanging onto Lucas's arm, and although he jumped, he was the furthest from the scene. Before he could get through, the monster was inside the elevator. It grabbed his ankle and held tight with octopus-like tentacles.

Todd screamed.

"It's got him!" yelled Lucas. "I can't pull him through!"

"Hold onto him!" screamed the girl. She snapped her fingers and a rope appeared. Quickly she tied the rope around Lucas and linked him to a nearby tree. "Don't let go!"

She stepped back into the elevator, her body shaking, and fear and disgust of the monster etched onto her face.

Todd, one arm into the scene held by Lucas and one leg in the black void, looked at her with blind panic. "Help me!" his hoarse voice whispered. "It's got me!"

The girl moved forward and softly stroked one tentacle of the monster in a loving fashion. She began to sing the song of marriage from long ago.

The tentacle slid from the boy's leg and slid back into the void. The monster face disappeared, and for a moment, Todd saw the likeness of a man in the doorway. The face was still horrible, but not quite as monstrous. The door shut and disappeared. The mirrored wall was back.

"Hurry," ordered the girl. "Into the picture before it realizes that I've tricked it!" She pulled Todd into the scene.

6

THE FUTURE

"Where are we?" asked Todd. The scene was like nothing he'd seen before.

"We are here," she answered simply.

Both boys frowned.

Lucas, stepping forward, said, "Who *are* you? What's happening to us? And like my friend said, 'Where are we?'"

The girl smiled. "So many questions. You are the same every time—but different."

"Here we go again," said Todd under his breath. "The same but different."

"First, I've been called many things. My first name was Anitra. This is the name that began all the pain. You ask what is happening to you. You have been caught in a family feud that has lasted many lifetimes. And, as I told your friend, you are here."   She raised her arms and glanced around, before looking back at the boys.

"That really hasn't told us much of anything," said Lucas softly while moving a step closer to her. "Back there in that elevator, back there—"

"Yes, I know. The monster."

"And I saw it turn into a man," added Todd. "An ugly devil, for sure, but a man just the same."

"Yes, that is true, too," agreed the girl.

"Please," said Lucas. "We were almost killed in there. Don't you think you owe us an explanation?"

"You will not remember it for very long," she said.

The boys frowned again.

Lucas persisted. "Still. I would like to know. I want to understand it all, if only for now."

"Very well," she replied. "Follow me to a place where we can talk."   She moved away from the boys, turned, and waited for them to follow.

Looking at each other, Todd and Lucas both raised their eyebrows.

Todd scratched his head. "We're in the matrix," he whispered.

Lucas smacked his arm. "Will you shut up about that movie?"

The boys followed. As they walked, they tried to take in their surroundings and to figure out exactly where they were. It was difficult.

The tree the girl had tied Lucas to had disappeared, just as the rope had, as soon as Todd had been pulled through to safety. The land was sandy, like a desert, with no visible vegetation anywhere; the sky an odd shade of yellow. There was nothing as far as the eye could see.

"So where are we going?" asked Todd. "We're not walking *toward* anything."

"Possibly the matrix," she said sweetly and smiled at him, not seeming to be bothered at all by the stark surroundings.

"Humph," he murmured. "Everybody's a comedian. I loved that movie—even if it's a hundred years old."

"Time doesn't matter," the girl said, a soft tone to her voice.

She was so angelic that Lucas fought taking in his breath. He wondered why he was feeling so strongly about someone he didn't know and who seemed so strange. This was not like him at all.

The next moment, there was a subway type entrance going down underground. It appeared to be made from concrete.

"That wasn't there before," remarked Lucas cautiously.

"Yes," she replied. "It was. You just did not see it."

Lucas shook his head at Todd. "It wasn't there," he whispered.

"No kidding," whispered Todd back.

The boys followed her down the stairs to a gloomy underground tunnel. Rats scurried along the edges of the walls and showed no fear as the trio approached.

"Nice place," mumbled Todd. He squinted to see where he was going.

"It is your destiny," she said.

"Oh great. My destiny? What does that mean?" asked Todd.

"Please wait," she asked. "We will talk soon. I must gather my thoughts."

"She needs to gather her thoughts," said Todd with sarcasm. "Ya think?"

Lucas nodded.

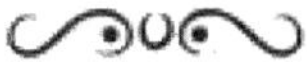

The monster was furious! It had been tricked by Anitra again! Shaking with fury, it floated in the Black Place, pounding and slamming against the crack each time it passed by it. Its anger kept growing and growing, and the taste for revenge smothered its desire for the girl.

It would not only kill the boy now, after the marriage, it would kill the girl, too. But only after the girl changed it back to the man it once was. Only after the curse was broken. Then she would be destroyed.

And the Dark Family would live. And it would spread evil again, far and wide, until every human was either evil or dead.

Sadness fell upon it for a moment. When the marriage music had reached its ears, just before the close of the door, it had become human-like again. It felt, for a brief moment, the feeling of love from so long ago. It could picture her in a gown with flowers at the hem. It could see its wife-to-be.

But she had cheated it with this nasty trick! She used the song promising marriage to free the boy's friend. She would pay. The boy would pay. The boy's friend would pay.

Everyone would pay! It slammed again against the crack in rage.

Then the monster floated again in swirling vengeful circles, and it waited. It always had one thing: Time. There was always time. And time would tell.

⌇

Lucas and Todd looked about with great interest, while they waited for Anitra to return.

"Beam me up, Scotty," said Todd.

Lucas shook his head. "Don't you ever stop? We're in serious trouble here. Or haven't you realized that yet?"

"I've realized. Trust me on that," replied Todd. "But I can't change. This is me, pal. It's how I hold together. How I cope without dying of friggin' fright. I have to be stupid and stuff."

"Yeah, right. Sorry. I'm edgy." Lucas felt as though every nerve of his body was at attention; it was a creepy sensation. He understood his friend's survival methods perfectly.

"Me, too." Todd was all too well aware of what *edgy* meant in the world of monsters.

"I mean, look at this place. What do you figure? The year 2050, 2060, something like that?" asked Lucas.

"Maybe," said Todd. "One thing's for sure: somebody pushed the panic button and kissed the world goodbye. That's nuclear destruction out there."

"Scary," said Lucas. "I never thought I'd see anything like this."

"Yes," the girl said, re-entering the space. "A dead world is scary. But many survived. You survived, Lucas."

"What about me?" asked Todd, eyes wide in question.

"I'm sorry," she apologized. "I really don't know anything about you. You are here only because Lucas wants you here."

Todd gave Lucas a sarcastic look to thank him. "Story of my life," he said.

"I don't understand any of this," said Lucas. "Maybe you better tell us."

"Yes," she began. "I will tell you, but should we survive, you will forget it all."

"No matter," he replied, "at least I'll know now. Start with the monster."

"The monster. Yes. The monster was once a human being many, many lifetimes ago in, what you call, medieval times. There were two families of magic back then, the dark and the light. I am from the Light Family. We practice good magic—the enchantment of love, health, and internal happiness." She turned her back to them and took a deep breath before speaking again. "Gunnar—the thing you saw as a monster—was a dark magician. He and his family practiced evil magic. But we both had to answer to the Creator, who has ruled our kind...forever. The Creator is the God you worship now in your time. In earlier times, the Creator became angry at the hate in the world and forced the song of marriage on our families. I was to marry the evil Gunnar of the Dark Family. This suited him and his family. He felt love—of a sort—for me, and our marriage would save his family from being cursed and forever kept in the dead, Black Place. You've had a look at that evil location."

Lucas nodded with a grimace on his face. No words were needed.

"Well, what happened?" asked Todd. "You chicken out, or something?"

She nodded. "Actually, I ran off with a young squire. Lucas of Lebaron. You, Lucas, in another life. We met when we were just sixteen, and though I barely knew you, I went with you when you asked me to marry you. I left Gunnar behind to face the Creator. And Gunnar and his family were banished to the Black Place—because of me."

"But how does that explain all this?" asked Lucas. "I've been dreaming about you—only the dreams aren't dreams! Everything is real! And my dreams aren't from medieval times, either!"

"I know. You are right. Your dreams are real. Each dream is a lifetime that you have lived with me. Your next question will be 'How?' My answer is: light magic. My magic allows me to meet you and live a life with you during each of your lifetimes. Wherever the Creator chooses to send you, I have the power to go there and be with you."

"You mean he has the same girlfriend in every life?" asked Todd.

The girl nodded.

"Bummer," mumbled Todd.

Lucas sat quiet, waiting for more of the story to be told.

"So, the monster in the Black Place is Gunnar. He can only break the curse by marrying me—and I will never do that. But the monster has become wise over the lifetimes. While you and I, Lucas, live our lives happily, one after another, the monster watches. The world has become a little more evil with each passing lifetime, and a crack has developed in the Black Place. A crack leading to the real world. The world where you now live."

"And the crack from the black world into ours is in the elevator," stated Lucas.

She nodded.

"How does it happen to be in the elevator that I work in?" Lucas shuffled about nervously. The explanation was causing more questions, and he wasn't feeling any better for knowing what was happening.

"The crack merely is the beginning of a doorway to the world. The monster chooses where it will enter." She stood quiet, waiting while he thought for a moment and asked a new question.

"What does it want from me?"

"It wants nothing from you, really," she said. "At least that was true before. It wants only to possess me. It means to do it by luring me to it using bait."

"And I'm the bait," said Lucas.

"Yes. And then, once it has me, it will barter. It will try to make me marry it by saying it will set you free. It will not. It will kill you. And in the end, after it has become human again, it will kill me. It thinks I do not know this, but my magic tells me this is the truth."

All went silent as Lucas and Todd digested the news. It wasn't what they wanted to hear.

"What can we do then?" asked Lucas, reaching forward to take her hand.

"Hold it!" said Todd. "What do you mean we? I ain't no Batman or even Superman's son or anything like that! How are we going to do anything to fix this?"

"You will go back and remember nothing," the girl said, looking gently into Todd's wide eyes. "Lucas and I must defeat the monster. We must if we are to live. This does not need to affect you, my funny friend."

"I was just kidding," Todd said quietly. "No way I'm gone leave my pal under these circumstances."

She nodded again.

"How?" asked Lucas. "You said it watches. If it knows what we're doing, won't it be prepared?"

"No," she answered. "We are in the future here. It cannot see into the future. Only its present and past. This is our future, and this time has not taken place yet. We can plan here."

"Oh," both boys said at the same time, but they frowned at each other.

"There is one thing I must tell you," she said softly.

"Uh, oh," said Todd. "Here comes the bomb."

Lucas swallowed hard. "What is it?"

To get back to your present, we have to travel through the Black Place."

"Boo, hiss!" sneered Todd. "I don't want to play this game anymore."

"Stick a sock in it!" whispered Lucas.

"It will learn that we've come to the future. It will search the past for our favorite lives together. And it will search our present."

"Great," said Todd. "Just great."

The girl looked steadily at Lucas. "It will not know we are coming. It would never think we would willingly go through the Black Place. It does not know that the only way to and from the future is through the blackness."

"The old element of surprise," said Todd. "Somehow it doesn't seem enough."

She ignored him and continued to stare into Lucas's frightened eyes. "This is the first time I've used the future. I knew someday it would be necessary, but I did not want to place you in danger with me. Forgive me, Lucas."

Lucas nodded and squeezed her hand.

The monster was still waiting. Agitation shook its body. It floated along the edges of the environment and looked and looked. Where was she? What deceit was this? This had not happened before.

She would disappear with him and then appear in another life. There were many. She liked to live the Seneca life again and again. And the days of the explorers. But she was not in either of those places—or anyplace else. Neither was the boy. It was as though she had disappeared...and that was impossible.

What had she done? Where had she gone? Did she know of the plan?

No! She could not. The evil was complete in the Black Place. The dark hid all truth. Nothing of the dark seeped through into the other worlds. Not yet. But it would.

It floated and waited. She would turn up, and she would pay.

But still, it searched.

7

MAJIC RATS

"I think I am going to die." Todd looked down at the stone-like plate before him. "Now I know I said I was hungry, but—"

"I'm really sorry, but as you can see, I have no control over the lifestyles in the places and times I live in. The major food of this time—your future and mine—is rat." The girl took a small bite of the roasted rat meat and made a sour face. "It's not that bad," but her tone was weak.

Lucas pushed his plate away. "I'm not really that hungry just yet."

"Give me yours, then," said Todd, pulling at Lucas's plate.

"I thought you just said you hated rat meat," remarked Lucas with a shake of his head.

"I do, but I have an idea. Pass me the pepper," instructed Todd. "And find me some foil, or Handiwrap, or a plastic bag, whatever—something to keep this garbage in."

"What's on your mind?" asked Lucas.

The girl slipped away to look for a wrapper.

"A little diversion," said Todd smugly. "Gunnar the Monstrous will be gunning for us when we go through the Black Place, right?"

Lucas nodded.

"And," continued Todd, "we—somehow—have to get through without getting eaten or torn apart or worse. Right?"

"Right." Lucas looked at Todd with renewed interest.

"Well, can you think of a better diversion than supplying a gourmet meal fit for monsters? Ratburgers! Hmmmmmmm! Come and get it!"

The girl returned with a plastic bag for the rats and Todd told her his idea.

"That's really a very good idea," she said.

"It is?" said Todd. "Do you mean you don't have a better one?"

"Not really." She shrugged and shook her head.

"Gee," he said. "I was hoping for a real plan." He peppered one of the rats heavily.

Lucas watched closely and then smiled. "I get it. One rat diverts the monster..."

"And the other rat," finished Todd, "stays with us, just in case we need it."

"I can toss the rat into the darkness at a place far from where we will enter," offered the girl. "We only have a short way to go through the black before we come out on the other side. Of course, once you reach Miladon, I won't be with you...But you should make it."

"Hold it," said Lucas, holding up one hand. "What do you mean, you won't be with us? And where is Miladon?"

"I get the feeling she's been working on a plan after all." A small smile took form on Todd's face. "Thank goodness."

"Yes, I have been thinking about this, and I think I have the answer—of a sort. *If* we can get through the Black Place alive."

"We're listening," said Lucas. He was leaning toward her, mesmerized by her, and hoping she had a good idea.

Todd continued to pepper the rat.

"Long ago," began the girl, "way before I was born, my family was created—put on earth by the Creator. Miladon was our home. As a gift to my newborn light-magic family, the Creator presented my ancestors with a jeweled dagger. This dagger has many powers. The Creator warned the family about using the dagger unwisely. It could cause the destruction of the world in the wrong hands.

"The Creator told them that it would be used for a special purpose one day, and all in the family would know when the time to use the dagger was right. They were told to guard it well. The family decided to bury the dagger away, where there would be no chance of someone using it for the wrong purpose and at the wrong time. It was buried deep in the Earth, in a place only known to the family of light in that time.

"The secret was never passed on. The story was told, but the whereabouts of the dagger remain a mystery."

"How come?" asked Todd. "How will it be found if it's needed? Shouldn't at least one person in each generation know? That's the way I woulda handled it. Not knowing can't be good. Think about it."

"This question was raised. But everyone from the original family knew that the secret need not be revealed. They would not say why. I know why now."

"Why?" asked Lucas. "This has to do with us, doesn't it? We need that dagger, don't we?"

"Yes. You must go back in time, Lucas. To the time before I was born. You can do that, for you have been living lives for as long as there has been time. My lifetimes were only created when my family came to life at the will of the Creator. The Creator gave us life—the family of the light. You have always been." She paused to sigh. "You must go back and get the dagger from my family. You must then live the life there past the time of my creation and up to my marriage day.

"And on that day, you must step forward and challenge Gunnar. You must kill him before he is banished. Then the Black Place will be gone, and Gunnar will have never been turned into the monster."

"I've never heard of this Creator who actually visited people and gave them daggers..." remarked Lucas.

"No. The specific religion is not recorded. It was planned that way. It is so with many religions. Only tidbits of facts...especially those of evil."

Todd perked up. "Like vampires and stuff?"

She nodded, and Todd just blinked, surprised by her agreement.

All three sat silent, lost in their own thoughts for a moment.

"You've got to be kidding. All this is crazy," Lucas finally said. "So, what's happening in my life back home while all this is going on? While I'm living this other life. And what about Todd? What happens to him?"

"This is magic," she reminded him. "There will be no loss of time from your present life—unless you fail. Then you will have never existed anyway. And Todd is also in the same kind of limbo at this point. He can join you, if he wishes. Or he can wait in the future to see how things go. Whatever happens, he can live his life here in peace."

"No way, Jose!" snapped Todd. "Living on ratburgers is not my idea of a vacation. I'm going along with you." He then moved away to scout for more pepper for his rat, and Lucas sat quietly talking with the girl.

"I don't even know what to call you," said Lucas softly.

"In each of my dreams, you had a different name for me—" she began. "My first given name was Anitra. All the other names are variations of the first one. You may call me Anitra, if you like," she said, lightly placing her hand over his. "I'm sorry this had to happen, Lucas. Our lives have been together since I was created, and I suppose running away from Gunnar all those lifetimes ago has brought us some real problems."

Lucas nodded but said nothing. There certainly were problems to deal with—only they weren't just run-of-the-mill problems. These were super-duper make-you-crazy kinda problems. Or kill ya problems. They were bad.

She was right about it, of course, but at the same time, he was glad he was there with her. He felt as though his life belonged tangled up with hers, even if it was a messy-mush kind of knotted affair. There was a happiness inside him now he'd never felt before. It was so weird—like it was real, but it wasn't.

He smiled, knowing Todd would get a kick out of that. Fear lurked in his heart, too, though, because he wasn't sure at all that he could handle any of it. He could end up dead along with Anitra and Todd. That wasn't good. Still, the happiness being near her smothered most of that.

"Everything's going to be all right," he finally said to her and touched her hand. "At least, I hope so." Lucas smiled.

Anitra blushed and looked down. "Maybe we should just stay in the future," she suggested. "We could be happy together here. It would never find us. At least, not for a very long time."

"You know we can't do that," said Lucas, now sliding his hand over her golden hair. He wondered briefly how she managed to change so from life to life, yet still seem the same in his heart. "Our time is in the past now—my present." He frowned but went on when he saw she understood what he meant. "And besides, Anitra, the monster would eventually find us. It may take it another hundred lifetimes, but we would have to fight this same battle at some point when things caught up."

"Yes," she agreed. "Yes, we would. The fight will come one way or one time or another." Her eyes looked sad.

Todd returned with more pepper.

"Okay," said Lucas. "Get ready to throw the rat!"

"I'm ready," Anitra said. "Remember we must move very quickly as soon as I throw it into the Black Place. It won't take the monster long to gobble it up and be after us."

"Maybe we'll be lucky, and it won't realize that we're going through," said Todd hopefully.

"No," said Lucas. "There's a strong feeling in me that says that thing is just waiting for us."

"The feeling is in me, too," agreed Anitra. "I'm sure, by now, the monster has found that it cannot find us in the past or your present. Yes, it's waiting for us. We won't have much time."

"Let's go, then," said Lucas. "Do we have all the supplies we need, Todd?"

"I think so." Todd rifled through the small pile on the floor. "The two rats, a rope, a knife for each of us—not much use against what I saw before to be honest—and more pepper."

The meat smelled delicious! The monster sniffed at it, being careful, getting close, before taking a lick with its thick, mossy tongue.

Rat meat!

Saliva dripped from the monster's mouth and its teeth glistened. Such a delicacy! In this place, it was not used to such a wonderful thing. Here, there was little to eat.

But where had the food come from?

The monster looked around quickly, peering into each dark corner of the Black Place. It ate the meat, tearing tiny pieces off and savoring the flavor. It would never do to swallow it in one lump. Savor it, savor it! Who knew when there would be more?

The monster thought of the girl and of the boy, too. Yes! That was it. The meat smelled of them! An offering of food did not come without reason. It floated through the Black Place. Agitated. They were up to something and it would expose their plan. They would not win this time.

"It's so dark in here," said Lucas, squeezing Anitra's hand. "Which way do we go?"

"Toward Kansas," whispered Todd. "I don't want to see the wizard in this movie."

"Shhhhh," hushed Lucas.

"See the pinpoint of light ahead?" Anitra pointed, her voice soft. "That is the past. It is a light meant only for us to see. My family knows you are coming!"

"How can that be possible?" asked Lucas, inching forward; he was filled with dread and sickness. The Black Place was terrible. The smell was like death, itself; and the floor felt slippery and slimy. He tried not to think about the reason for the slime.

Anitra huddled close to him. "I told you before. My family has waited for this moment. They know you will be coming for the dagger. In their hearts, they know!"

"I just stepped in dog crap...or something," whispered Todd. "Ugh."

Lucas ignored his friend and pushed forward toward the light. The faster they moved, the better. The Black Place overloaded his senses. One minute he felt hot and muggy, as though he were in a jungle; then a cold and damp chill would rush through his body, making him shiver. Lucas knew the others felt it, too.

Anitra hung close and Todd was continually mumbling.

They heard it. The monster's breath, loud and raspy, and seeming to be in the very air about them. And it was getting closer.

Lucas hurried the group along, keeping their backs to one slippery wall. Despite the closeness of the light now, his heart raced with fear. At any moment, he expected the monster to jump out at them and tear them to pieces.

He stopped, and was nearly knocked down when Todd smacked into him.

"Something's happening," whispered Lucas. "Hold up!"

"Whoa!" said Todd, grabbing hold of Anitra. "Ewww! Don't touch the wall, whatever you do."

The open area in front of them was reshaping itself. Now the light from the past seemed to be at the end of a longer corridor—twice as far away as it should have been.

"Oh no!" cried Anitra. "It knows we're here. It has seen us and is changing the Black Place to confuse our minds!"

"As if we need more confusion," mumbled Todd, looking around and testing the floor with his foot. "The floor's turned mushy. That can't be good."

"I know," said Lucas. "And that's not the worse. Look toward the light. The new hallway is sloping upward."

The corridor was now a sharp incline. There would be no way to move up that hall without hand or foot grips. The light was slipping further and further away.

"We must do something now!" said Anitra. "If the light disappears, then we will have lost our chance! And we will never find our way back to the future! We'll be stuck here, and then dead."

"Give me the supplies," ordered Lucas. "The rope, I need the rope!"

Todd threw the whole bag at Lucas. "I'm keeping my knife, pal."

Lucas merely nodded and turned toward Anitra. Even in the dark, there was a glow about her. This glow was the only thing allowing the group to see at all in the Black Place. For a moment, he was lost for words. She was so beautiful.

Anitra touched Lucas's cheek softly to bring his thoughts back to the danger at hand.

He jumped at her touch.

"You said they knew we were coming?" he said.

"Yes."

"If I toss this rope toward that light, will it make it through into that past world? And will they pull us out? Is this place really changed or does it just look like it's changed?"

"I don't know," answered Anitra. "I think that the rope will be drawn to the light, just as we are. Do you feel the pull? And if that's so, maybe we will be pulled up this hallway. We can only try."

"Whatever you're gonna do, do it now!" snapped Todd. "We can't stay here! The breathing is getting louder, and I think that thing is just playing cat and mouse with us!"

"He's right," said Anitra. "Throw the rope! It's our only hope!"

Lucas tied one end of the rope around his waist and hurled the rest of it up the long passage.

They watched the rope float along, as if being pulled, toward the light. In another few seconds, the rope was at the light and then through it.

"This place is messing with our minds!" said Lucas. "The hall seems much longer than it really is. The rope should've never even reached the light yet!"

He gently tugged at the rope and it felt secure. He jerked harder. The rope held.

"Okay, let's go!" he said, pushing Anitra before him on the rope and then Todd.

"Here," Todd started up the rope, "hold my rat."

"What I always wanted," mumbled Lucas, taking the bag.

The trio inched toward the light.

8
BELIEVE!

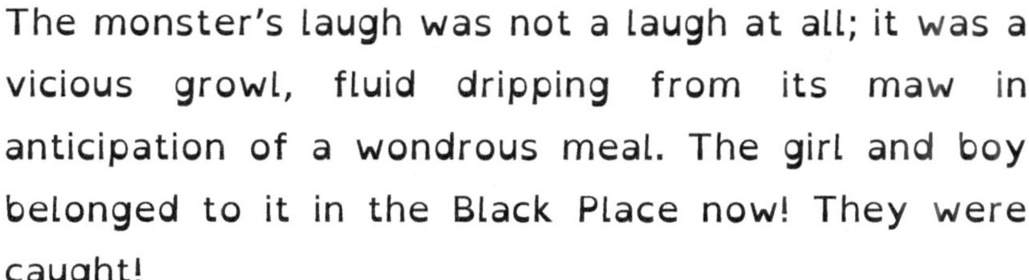

The monster's laugh was not a laugh at all; it was a vicious growl, fluid dripping from its maw in anticipation of a wondrous meal. The girl and boy belonged to it in the Black Place now! They were caught!

It floated closer, thinking how stupid the girl was. An offer of rat meat was not enough to gain entrance to the past! How could she think it so dumb to fall for a trick that a child constructed? For all of them were just that—children. Bad children! It would have their lives this time! Its bellowing rang through the darkness like a misshapen bell.

For now, though, it played with them—shaping and reshaping the Black Place to confuse the travelers. What fun it was having. There had not been such activity in a very long time...it paused in its triumph...no, there'd never been activity in this place, much less this luscious edible kind.

It thought itself so clever. It made the rooms of its home hot and then cold and the floors mushy and wet. This would surely disgust them and take their attention from whatever they were planning. It swirled and laughed, stirring up a cloud of toxic gas to add to the mix. This was such fun!

But then it was startled.

They had thrown a rope into the past.

The past? That was not possible...unless there was a power from that time listening in. And how could that be? There was no link that allowed it.

Why, it had taken time immortal to open the crack in the elevator. Nothing from the past could do the same. Nothing from the past could catch a rope. Nothing in the past could ruin its plans...The monster floated more quickly.

Maybe it had been wrong...too confident in its own game. Playtime was over, and it was hungry for the boy. There was no more thrill of the chase. Those times were over now. This boy and his friend would make a wonderful marriage feast. And the girl would watch it all.

The three travelers were close to the light now. It seemed quite bright and not far from their reach. Yet...it seemed always just out of range.

"Come on!" Lucas' whisper rasped. "Climb faster, I hear something behind us! And you know what that's gotta be! It can't be as far to the light as it looks!"

At that moment and just as Anitra reached the light, the monster burst from the deep darkness and snapped at the rope, breaking it. The three began to tumble back—into the monster's waiting jaws.

It howled with delight, filling the place with such painful noise that their ears began to bleed.

"Hold on!" yelled Anitra. "Don't let it fool you! We are at the light! Don't fall back! It's just an illusion that it has made for us. Believe in the light!"

Anitra, realizing the magic of the place, seemed to stand on flat ground in mid-air while Todd and Lucas tottered downward. She held out her hand to Todd, who was nearest.

"Take my hand and stand with me!" she commanded him.

Todd grabbed her and then lunged for Lucas's hand, catching it just before Lucas would slip into the monster's drooling mouth. The boys hung with their feet dangling in open space; the floor was no longer under them.

Anitra, however, stood on invisible solid ground just before the light and with enough strength to easily hold them fast. "Believe!" she screamed. "You must believe! See me standing here! Look at me! I can hold both of you easily, but eventually you will fall if you don't believe! Look at me! If I can do it, so can you!"

Lucas looked up at Todd and then back into the monster's mouth, his heart pounding at the thought of the sharp teeth crunching down on him. Then he remembered the bag still held in his other hand: the rat, Todd's peppered rat! He tossed the bag into the monster's open mouth and then grabbed Todd with both hands.

The monster, at first, took the new offering of rat meat happily. But then, as the pepper filled its throat all at once and not in small pieces, a rage took over. Its tongue and throat burned from the hot meal and it grew weak with the buildup of air collecting in its lungs.

"That's 'a one spicy meatball!" yelled Todd in his best Italian accent.

The floor came back beneath the boys' feet, relieving Anitra's need to hold them so tightly. But the air around them was disappearing.

The monster was sucking every bit of it into its lungs because of the pepper. It sneezed, a great nasal eruption, splattering the three with slime, blowing them out of the Black Place and into the light.

"We made it!" yelled Todd, tumbling into the past.

"Thank God!" said Lucas with a sigh, rolling behind him.

The monster bellowed and roared. Its anger shook the Black Place, and each of the worlds it knew felt the earthquakes marking that roil of emotion. It would not give up this easily. It would wait. It would always wait.

This wasn't over.

But what had been Anitra's plan? Lucas felt her loss. She was gone now, and he was alone with his Todd. What was her plan?

He really wished she'd told him.

Lucas looked down at the brown tunic and tights he wore and whistled. "Wow," was all he could manage before he glanced at Todd, who looked like a skinny beanstalk dressed all in green. A giggle escaped despite their dire circumstances.

Todd wrinkled his nose and looked around.

"If you even think to mention that this isn't Kansas," said Lucas, "I'm going to come over there and smack you."

"I wasn't!" defended Todd, scrambling to his feet and brushing himself off. "Actually...I was going to say, 'ALL FOR ONE, AND ONE FOR ALL.' You know, the Mousekateers and all that stuff?"

Lucas shook his head, pulling himself to his feet also. "The Musketeers," he corrected. "And that was in the seventeenth century. We're way further back than that. Look over there," he pointed. "That castle is from medieval times, at least. Remember what Anitra said about this place."

Off in the distance, the boys could see the foggy outline of a huge stone-like castle. Its dreariness set the stage for knights with shining armor and damsels in distress. They were on the edge of a forest overlooking a vast open field dotted with little shacks. People dressed in peasant clothes were working in the fields.

The boys stepped back to the cover of the woods.

"She's gone," remarked Lucas, somewhat aware now of his surroundings. "I can't believe it. She was with us in the Black Place, and now she's gone."

"Well, I can believe it," answered Todd, dropping down hard to the ground and leaning his back against a tree. "Notice that our friendly neighborhood monster is also missing." He began to sing a song his little brother always sang while watching Sesame Street—changing a word or two. "Who are the monsters in your neighborhood? In your neighborhood, in your neigh-bor-hood, Ohhhh—"

"Knock it off," said Lucas, but only slightly agitated. It was a good thing to know the monster was left behind for the time being. "We've got to get a plan together here. We've got to find this dagger and high tail it back to our present."

"Yeah," agreed Todd, "but how are we going to find her family? Where do we start?"

"I guess at that castle." Lucas started back out of the woods and down the field toward the structure. "Come on!" he called back.

Todd plodded wearily behind him. "This is going to be a long day; I just know it."

Lucas was mildly confused,, and even a bit frightened by the reactions of the workers in the field as they approached. When the people saw them, they all ran to hide inside their little shacks.

Todd called into a few of the homes, but no one would answer. He banged on their doors and tried to enter but each door was bolted from the inside.

"Strange people around here," he said to Lucas.

"Yes, and I don't think this is a good sign. Remember, it's us who are the strangers..."

Once they began to ignore the behavior of the workers, it didn't take them long to reach the castle. It loomed above them, dark and cold, with tall stone walls protecting it from outsiders. A moat circled the property, making the draw bridge the only entrance.

It was a stereotypical dark castle to be sure and the boys hesitated before walking in.

"May the force be with you," whispered Todd, pushing Lucas forward.

Lucas gave Todd a frown and walked across the bridge.

There was an uncomfortable sensation of shifting wood, squeaking from extensive use, and they had to be even more careful because some of the planks were missing. It would not take much to misstep and find themselves in the water below. They quietly moved forward.

Just inside the castle walls was a large courtyard with small lean-to stalls set up to sell and trade goods. The area smelled of grease and horse manure.

Beyond this marketplace was the castle itself, a frightening building full of shadows and mystery.

"This place looks like it would fit very nicely into a really scary horror movie," whispered Lucas.

"Yeah, how about *The Invasion of the Castle Monsters*, or something equally out of this friggin' world," suggested Todd.

Lucas smiled thinly and looked about the marketplace. A few merchants peddled their goods, but for the most part, the stalls stood deserted, as though left behind in a hurry. The people still there stared coldly at the boys.

"Now what?" asked Todd. "Can't stay around here...these people look like they would tar and feather us in a heartbeat."

But Lucas did not have to answer. Just then a woman came through the tall iron castle doors and moved toward them. She was dressed entirely in black, with her face was covered with a dark veil. Eyes, also black and peering out above the shroud, were the only visible part of her body. And those eyes were dark and evil.

"We welcome you to the Family of the Dark," she said sternly.

Lucas and Todd both took their breaths in. Somehow, they had found their way to the Dark Family and not the Light Family where the dagger was!

"You come to amuse us at the celebration?" she asked, beckoning them to follow her to the castle.

The boys looked at her in confusion, but followed, not knowing what else to do.

"Yes," said Todd without thinking.

The woman nodded. "You look like jesters."

Todd stuck his tongue out at her back.

Lucas spoke up, "Actually, my friend here is the jester. I am merely a lost..." His voice trailed off. A lost what?

"Traveler?" she suggested, turning to look at him. "No. A squire. You have deserted your master." She sighed, the sound heavy, but almost approving. "I can always tell these things."

Lucas said nothing. He didn't know what a squire was or whether it was wise to have deserted a master. But it didn't sound good.

She laughed and dismissed his silence. "No matter. It has been long since we have had a handsome young man to look at. We still welcome you."

"Thank you." Lucas a forced smile.

"I will show you to your rooms." She strode toward a narrow stairway going down into the bowels of the castle. "Though we welcome you, we do not have separate sleeping areas for you. You must share at night as you have shared in journey."

The boys followed quietly as she took them down the winding stone steps. The air became stale and cold the further down they went.

Lucas tried to think. Could the Dark Family know what they were up to? Had they fallen into a trap? Still, they walked downward, not knowing what else to do.

Todd smacked him on the back. with urgency, but he just turned to shush him quietly and quickly, eyes wide as if to say, "I know, I know!"

The stairs finally leveled off, and they stood on the dirt floor of a large open area. Several stone doors were on either side.

"How rude of me," began the woman, turning to them. "I have not introduced myself to you. I am Drucil, sister of the great warrior Gunnar of the Dark." She walked to the last door and pushed it open. It squealed on rusty hinges.

Lucas and Todd glanced at each other with a look that said, "Oh no!"

"And you?" Ushering them into the unlit, dark room, she moved forward and lit several candles at once by merely snapping her fingers.

Todd was at a loss for words.

Lucas stepped forward and nodded to her. "I am Lucas of Bellington." He used the hotel as his last name.

"I," said Todd, finding his voice, "am Todd of Bellington."

Lucas frowned at him, wondering why he also chose the hotel. It would not do for people here to think they had too much in common.

The woman nodded and left them. "You will be called for later. Rest for now."

"This is just great!" said Todd sarcastically, after the woman left. "That woman is the monster's sister! Talk about 'out of the frying pan and into the fire' scenarios."

"Yes," agreed Lucas. "I don't know how things could go worse than this."

"Now why did you have to say that?" Todd said with exasperation. "You know what happens when people say that. Things get worse. Always and without exception, things get worse."

The boys walked cautiously around the room. It was a cold place, full of shadows and small darting shapes. There were two bedding areas that appeared unclean and possibly poisonous with the varied varmints and insects.

"This place has rats," Lucas pointed, noticing their scurrying bodies at the edges of the walls.

"I'll never say a bad thing about a rat as long as I live," remarked Todd, thinking of the monster in the Black Place and the spicy rat that had saved their lives.

"Me neither, but I still don't care to live with them. This place feels so unsafe and lonely. It reminds me of a dungeon. Not that I've ever been in a dungeon, but it's like I think it might feel." Lucas shivered, looking at the beds of straw in a far corner. "How do you think people managed to survive in this time?"

"Guess you can get used to anything," said Todd. "I mean, look how we live. Think these guys could get used to McDonalds?"

"What are you talking about? I can't get used to McDonalds," said Lucas not more than a whisper.

"Hey. Careful now. I love me a Big Mac." Then he paused, his muscles tensing. "Wait, listen." The faraway sound of footsteps could be heard moving swiftly toward their room.

"Like I said before," Lucas began, swallowed hard and then added, "things couldn't get worse. Could they?"

The footsteps stopped outside the door to the boys' room and the heavy stone door began to swing inward, squealing against the rusty hinges again.

"Nails on a blackboard!" said Todd, gritting his teeth at the sound.

Lucas nodded and whispered to himself, "Things couldn't get worse, things couldn't get worse..."

Then, in the open doorway, stood a dark shadow of a man. He moved into the room and glared at the boys, and they could see he was not a man to cross.

His eyes were as black as Drucil's, and his clothes suggested that he was a wealthy and proud part of the castle. His full, swinging cape reminded Lucas of Dracula, and the eyes were surely just as evil.

But the worst was the man's face. Half was to some degree normal, but the other half was deformed and ugly. It was as though the man had survived a terrible fire...or something worse. The ugliness was distressing; it was difficult not to cringe and pull back.

Lucas swallowed hard again but remained silent and still. It would do them no good—in fact, it could harm things—were they to appear frightened.

"Well," said the man in a harsh tone, "news has reached me that we have our jester and a visitor, as well."

The boys nodded, not taking their eyes from the man.

"I am Lord Gunnar of the Dark Family," said the man holding his head high.

"Things just got worse," mumbled Todd.

9

SURELY YOU JEST...

"Do I know you, boy?" demanded Gunnar, looking at Lucas coldly. Both the man's eyes were strange—they appeared to move in different directions and there was a glow to them that made the black look blacker than black—almost purple. "I could swear I know you."

"No sir," Lucas almost stumbled over the words as they tumbled across his tongue, trying not to look him in the eyes. "I am a lost traveler. A squire. I became separated from my master, and I am anxious to find him again. I am Lucas of Bellington."

Gunnar stood very still and stared at Lucas without speaking. His black eyes seemed to tear into Lucas's flesh, and for a moment, Lucas felt that the evil Gunnar would strike out at him, recognizing him from some other time and place—even possibly from the Black Place, but that was impossible. Wasn't it? He couldn't know him from a time before there was a time, could he? That didn't even make sense to Lucus's own brain as he thought it. But things seemed to be okay.

Instead of attacking him, the man wiped away the dripping fluid from one of his bad eyes and turned his stare to Todd.

"You look very much like a jester," he remarked, a nasty edge to his tone. "I hope you will make us laugh. Others before you have met their fate for not amusing us."

Cold sweat drizzled down the skin on Todd's back; he knew that this was no exaggeration. That could be felt in the aggression of his tone. "I'll do my best," he said, sorry now that he'd accepted that title in the first place.

Gunnar turned back to Lucas. "You will join us at the celebration feast before you continue your search for your master. I need to think about you a bit. I know that you've crossed my path before. I just can't seem to..."

Trying to change the direction of Gunnar's thoughts, Lucas asked, "What are you celebrating Lord Gunnar?"

Gunnar's harshness disappeared momentarily. "Ah yes! What am I celebrating, you ask? My upcoming marriage, young peasant! But I doubt you know of these things—you with your lowly upbringing. You with no magic to offer or understand! No princess for you! Eh?"

He stopped and seemed to fall into a dream state before continuing. "My marriage to the lovely Anitra of the Light Family. I celebrate the end of distress for my family. The marriage will see them safe for all time. Just a little good mixed in and all eternity is ours!" He laughed, the wicked sound filling the room and echoing off the walls.

The boys remained silent, afraid of Gunnar and frozen by the insane laughter that seemed to bounce about the room. This man—or whatever he was—certainly had the same vibrations as the monster in the Black Place. No mistaking that once the laughter escaped his mouth.

"Rest well for a short time," instructed Gunnar when his good mood passed. "Then follow the steps up to the main hall. Someone will show each of you to your special place in the ceremony." Gunnar turned to leave.

"Will your lady, Anitra, be at the celebration?" asked Lucas casually.

Gunnar spun around and glared at the boy. "She will not. This celebration is a family matter. Any other questions, boy?" Gunnar's nostrils flared and his hypnotic evil eyes were wide.

"No," said Lucas shrugging. "Just asking..."

"He was just asking," piped in Todd softly.

Gunnar smirked at them and the turned and left, leaving the heavy door open. His steps disappeared up the stairway.

Todd banged his hand on his head. "I can't believe this! We are going to die, pal. There's no other solution out of this. We are going to die. On our way out. Swimmin' with the fishes. Over, done with, sayonara, baby. Elvis has *left* the room."

"Hang tight!" snapped Lucas. "Keep your senses! We've got to get out of here!"

"Ya think? I'm all for that! And just how do we do that? Just walk up to the Dragon Lady and say, 'Hey, it's been nice, but I don't eat flies for lunch?' Or maybe we could go up to the great Lord Gunnar the Monstrosity and tell him we're late for an important date with his upcoming bride!"

"Stop," said Lucas softly. "I've got to think. There's got to be a way around all this. I mean, Anitra is not supposed to even be in the picture right now. How has this happened?"

"That's right," remembered Todd. "She's not supposed to be born yet. We were going to have to live up to that point and beyond until we could meet up with her."

"If she's already here, why didn't she come out of the Black Place with us?" asked Lucas.

"You're the resident expert on this whole mess. You tell me. And don't jesters have to have a hat and stuff?" remarked Todd. "How am I gonna pull that off? Everybody knows there nothing funny about me. I'm just...me. And that's all. Nada. Nothing else." He was shaking his head, the fear in his eyes shadowed only by his shaking hands.

Lucas shook his head. "I just don't know. But I do know that we've got to get out of here and get that dagger before this marriage takes place."

"Well, let's go upstairs out of this dungeon. We'll never get out of here sitting in this rat hole!" Todd offered, then added to the running creatures with them, "sorry rats, no hard feelings."

"Good idea. And Todd," Lucas said, "I hope you have something in mind for your clown act for these people. I know you don't really see yourself as a comedian, but...well, we just might have to go through with this celebration with them—if things don't go right. And they don't seem to be..."

"No way. You're trippin' dude," said Todd. "We get out *now*! Somehow. Some way. Out. Now."

"Yes, I agree. But if something goes wrong..."

Todd swallowed hard and answered, "I see your point. I suppose an old *Simpsons* routine would be wasted on these guys, huh?"

"I think so."

The boys headed out of their room, down the hall, and up the stairs toward the main hall. There was just no other choice.

⁓ↄʊɕ∾

Standing just outside the main hall by the stairway to the dungeons, the boys felt discouraged. The room was a flurry of activity and the front entrance to the courtyard was guarded by a tall, ugly-looking fat man. He was twice the size of Lucas and Todd together.

Gunnar stood with his sister, Drucil, at one end of the hall, shouting orders at every passing servant.

The boys slid back into the hallway and hunkered down in a corner to one side.

"We'll never get out this way," said Lucas. "There's too many people around. And I don't feel like running into Gunnar and Drucil again—even casually. Dangerous stuff. Especially if he ever 'remembers' my connection to his intended wife."

Todd nodded. "I'm not too interested in going out into that crowd, either. Notice anything else strange about them? I mean, like how they treat each other?"

"Yeah," answered Lucas. "Not real nice to each other, are they? And I don't think they take kindly to strangers." He now motioned Todd down a nearby passageway and away from the crowd. "We'll have to find another way."

"Ya know, in all the movies I've seen, these castles all have hidden passages and stuff like that," suggested Todd.

"I was thinking the same thing. And not only in movies. Things like that are historically sound for the times. I read that somewhere in class. Now we just have to find one of those passages. Or we may even find another way out. Let's follow this tunnel for a ways and see where it leads us. If we get caught, we can just say we were looking around and got lost. That sounds reasonable, right?" Lucas tried not to let his doubts seep into his voice.

Lit torches were set in holders every few feet, lighting their way, but even so, the smoke from the long sticks stung their eyes and made the walk uncomfortable. Todd sneezed and Lucas just gave him a dirty look. Although the tunnel was wide, the ceiling hung low and the boys' heads nearly touched the stone overhead. Any taller and they would have had to walk stooped over.

"I'm glad we don't live in these times," said Todd. "Or that I'm not taller."

Lucas nodded, but put his finger to his lips to quiet his friend. "Be careful; we don't know who could be listening. Who knows where this passage leads? It has to come out somewhere. Get into character just in case." He paused. "Well, do what you can with that, anyway."

Each keeping to one side and glancing back from time to time, they found that the corridor was becoming colder as they moved further into the castle. The dampness seemed to seep into their bones, and both boys shivered. The floor sloped downward. Before too long, the tunnel emptied into a small room with two open doorways leading away.

"Which way?" asked Todd, trying to catch his breath.

"Let's go to the right. That would be the way toward the front of the castle. We at least have seen the front and know our way around a little."

Lucas sighed, knowing that his statement was mostly untrue. He didn't know anything about the front of the castle beyond that it had a moat and some little rinky-dink carts.

Moving down the right-side of this new passage, the boys noticed right away how narrow the walkway was becoming. They could still move freely, but it had to be single file. The light was dimmer than it had been in the main tunnel, torches spread more thinly now, and the air was stale with a rotting smell to it. A growling sound came in echoes from further along the tunnel.

"Uh, oh," said Todd. "I don't like the sound of that...We better turn back. I think we're interrupting someone's dinner."

"We can't turn back," replied Lucas. "We have to move forward. You know what's behind us."

"Yeah, but we don't know what's in front of us, and it doesn't sound good at all," countered Todd.

Still, Todd followed Lucas reluctantly. What would they see beyond the next corner? Neither boy wanted to know. But there was no other way.

Finally, at the corner, Lucas pushed Todd against the wall behind him, holding him back with one arm, and peeked around. A glowing light falling from a doorway off the tunnel revealed another room.

"Something's in that room," whispered Lucas. "We both heard it."

"It's quiet now, though. What do you think it was?" asked Todd. "Could it have gone?"

"Anything's possible with this Dark Family," answered Lucas. "It can't be good, though, one way or another. Let's check it out."

"I'll wait here," said Todd.

"Come on!" said Lucas, pulling at Todd's tunic. "Don't be a chicken."

"Bawk, bawk, bawk," clucked Todd in a whisper, Lucas dragging him along.

Just then a robed figure rushed out of the lighted room and stood in the center of the tunnel, smelling the air and looking into every shadow. The figure started towards where the boys were hunkered down, hiding, when a loud clang boomed out from the far side of the tunnel.

Lucas peeked around just in time to see the figure raise his robe with one hand and yell out strange words. A new doorway appeared in a wall that had been stone one moment before. The figure walked through the doorway, and both the stone door and person disappeared.

Todd leaned over Lucas's shoulder. "Good trick. Let's get out of here! If these guys can do that kind of stuff—"

"Don't you see, Todd?" Lucas interrupted and shook him by the shoulders. "We can't just take off. If we don't go through with this, there's no future. There won't be any Todd or Lucas—or Anitra! No one will be alive. Everything will be gone. There's no turning back. Now come on!"

Todd nodded and blew air out his mouth in a loud sigh. "Forced to be a hero," he whispered. "Story of my life."

They crept forward and into the lighted room. At first, the boys saw nothing but a table filled with bottles, odd-looking kinds of vegetation, and dead animal parts.

"Looks like a laboratory of some kind," remarked Lucas, peering closely at the table. Then he jumped back, knocking Todd against a wall. "Uhhh!"

"What is it?" cried Todd, grabbing Lucas's arm in fear. "What?"

"A dead snake," answered Lucas, gathering his senses again. "It was just a dead snake. Sorry. It was dead, though, so we're good."

"You and your snakes," snapped Todd. "Here we fight monsters and travel through past lives and eat rats for lunch, and you get the shakes over a little snake. And a dead one no less."   Todd stepped forward and looked down at the dead animal. "Yuk. That's gross, though. They've torn off its head. Wonder why? Who would tear off the head of a snake? And why might be the better question…"

"Which is what will happen to us, should you decide to dally much longer!" said a clear voice from a dark corner in the room.

Both boys jumped back, their muscles tensing for a fight. The room fell silent. Their eyes gradually became used to the light and could finally make out the figure of a man, dressed entirely in white, chained to the wall.

"Can you see me now?" The man asked patiently.

"Yes," said Lucas, stepping forward. "Who are you, and why are you chained?"

Todd was gazing at the chains. "Looks just like a Dracula movie."

"There is no time for questions now," said the man. "My patience is limited in this evil place. Only know that I am your friend, and I know your mission. Come, release me."

Lucas walked forward and examined the chains. "What mission, old man?"

The man sighed. "Anitra."

That was enough for Todd. "Okay, he's a friend. Let's get him loose. He can help us get out. The more the merrier, I always say. When it comes to rescue missions, I mean."

Lucas watched the man carefully, taking in the crystal blue of his eyes and the strength in his face. This man resembled his love, Anitra.

He sucked in a long, deep breath. This was the first time he had admitted to himself how strong his feelings were for Anitra. But, of course, they must've been. After all, he was risking his life to save her from the powerful and evil Lord Gunnar.

Lucas relaxed in one way, but felt anguish in another. "I can't get you out of these chains, mister. There's not even a keyhole."

"Of course, there's no keyhole. The chains are magic," explained the man. "Use the power."

Todd moved closer now. "The power? You've got 'the power'?" He nudged Lucas.

"Yes," said the man. "You are in our time now. You are the chosen. You have the power of the Light Family. Use it wisely. Release me now, boy."

Lucas looked at Todd with raised eyebrows and then looked around the room behind him. "Power? Chosen?"

"Release him," said Todd with a crazed giggle. "Come on, Lucas, knock my socks off. Do the power!" Todd was worried by his own outburst. He sounded like a lunatic.

Lucas, without hesitation, turned back to the man, raised his arm and dropped it sharply, like he'd seen the man do in the hallway earlier. He added, "You are free!"

The chains holding the man disappeared. He rubbed his wrists and shook his legs. "Thank you, young man. I could not use the power with both my hands and legs chained. You are a good boy. Worthy of the White."

"Now I've seen everything," said Todd. "This is really getting crazy. No. I'm surely getting crazy."

"Come!" said the man. "We must leave here quickly. The black wizard will return!" He pointed his finger at Todd, "You! Stop being strange. Come, leave with us before you are eaten."

With that, he rushed from the room back into the tunnel.

"Wait!" cried Lucas. "There's nothing back that way in the tunnel and—"

The man silenced Lucas with a finger to his lips and then spread his arms across the tunnel wall. A doorway appeared.

"Now, ya know? That's really handy," said Todd. "I'm with him."

The three slipped through the door, and as they did, it disappeared behind them.

"Is this what they call the point of no return?" whispered Todd. "Who is this guy, anyway?"

"Good question," Lucas said to Todd. Turning to the old man, he said, "Do we have time to talk?"

"Yes," replied the man. "We are safe for a short time. But only a short time. We must find the White One and leave this castle before we are found and taken."

The boys frowned. "Who are you?" asked Lucas.

"I am Merek. Anitra's grandfather. Things have not gone right for you, and I have come to bring you back to the Light Castle. Unfortunately, I was found in the tunnels. Quite by accident, I might add. The White One and I were separated. While I searched, I neglected to pay attention to my surroundings; I was anxious, you see. I was worried. I walked right into the dark wizard's hall. It is an unforgivable mistake. I don't know how I will forgive myself." The man was very distressed by the error.

"No problem," said Lucas, trying to soothe the man's feelings. "We came by and everything is okay now."

"No, we still have a journey before we reach the dagger. And the wedding is tomorrow. We must hurry now!" Again, he began to move away from the boys.

"Wait a minute!" cried Lucas. "What do you mean the wedding is tomorrow? We were supposed to land in a time way before Anitra was born. She didn't come through with us. And this dark guy is talking weddings already. Tomorrow? Hell no."

Merek grew agitated, wanting to go quickly from the castle. "You were blown with great strength from the Black Place. Greater than we'd anticipated. Anitra moved right to the time of her birth, but you flew past her birth and did not fall from the Black Place until this time. The time of her marriage. We must hurry!"

"You mean Anitra is here? I'll be able to see her?" asked Lucas with excitement.

"Have you forgotten your mission, boy?" asked Merek. "I understand your feelings for her. It has always been this way for the two of you. But you must put all that aside now. Your life and hers—and that of everyone else's—depend upon you. You must have the dagger and destroy Gunnar before the marriage takes place!"

"Let's go then," said Lucas, pushing forth into the new tunnel. "Who is this White One you spoke of?"

"The White One is the powerful one. The White One leads and teaches our family. The White One has been with us always. The Creator gave us this teacher in the very beginning. The White One passes on our beliefs and teaches our young."

Todd shrugged. "Let's find him, then." He shivered. "It's cold here."

"Yes," agreed the man. "The new coldness tells me that the wizard has noticed my absence. Your absence will also be discovered soon. We must go!"

"Now, can we be the three musketeers?" whispered Todd in Lucas's ear.

Lucas pushed Todd hard enough to tumble him into Merek.

"Sorry," said Todd, tipping an imaginary hat.

The man stopped and smiled patiently at Todd. "You might be interested to know that one day you will be a musketeer of sorts."

"Yeah?" said Todd and threw his shoulders back. "Imagine that."

Lucas shook his head at his friend and then thought of Anitra. He sighed hard and followed Todd and Merek down the tunnel. What else could he do?

10

NOT SLIMY!

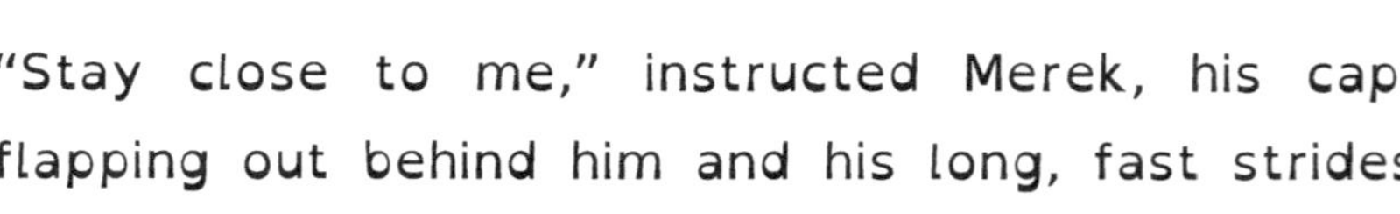

"Stay close to me," instructed Merek, his cape flapping out behind him and his long, fast strides. "There are many dangers in the tunnels." He had already taken them through four magic doorways into four new tunnels.

One tunnel had led to a room filled with sleeping scorpions the size of small horses. They'd slowly backed out and closed the room. Even Merek was breathing hard after that one. "One touch—not a sting—one touch would have put us in a black hell we'd never return from," he'd said.

The wizard's magic mesmerized Todd. "How come you can make doors in the walls and Lucas can make chains disappear with the drop of an arm?" asked Todd, keeping close behind the old man.

"It is our magic. This is a magic time. And the two of you have entered the Light Family. Therefore, you are magic, as well."

Todd frowned and looked back at Lucas.

Lucas shrugged.

A loud animal sound roared on the other side of the tunnel wall, making the two boys jump back against the opposite wall.

"What was that?" cried Todd. "It sounded terrible!"

"The Dark Family is searching for us in these tunnels. Stay quiet. Their monsters may hear us. They have very good ears and a great sense of smell. We are not safe."

"Don't have to tell me twice," whispered Todd, plastering himself against the cold wall.

Lucas pushed his way by Todd to the old man's side. "How do we find the White One with all these confusing passages and those evil things chasing us?"

"The White One will find us. Soon. We will hear."

"Oh," whispered Lucas, not understanding but frightened of the new sounds he was hearing from beyond the walls just as his friend was.

"We must not take or make a wrong tunnel," the man continued quietly. "If we are not careful, we might move into the Dark Family's path and meet the face of those fiendish sounds you hear."

"No problem," Todd whispered smartly. "If that happens, I'll just—" And he threw up his arm and waved it across the tunnel wall.

The wall immediately disappeared, replaced by a doorway and a huge black face with dripping teeth and fire eyes. It rushed through the door at them. The body, dragon-like and winged, smacked into Todd, knocking him against the far wall of the tunnel. It snapped its teeth, aiming for Todd's throat. He screamed and ducked beneath its wing.

Lucas lunged for Todd, pulling him from the monster's path just before he was trampled and the tunnel where they'd been seconds before was sprayed with fire from the thing's burning eyes.

The old man threw up both arms and bellowed at the monster, "*Ana Runu Belet!*" The monster crumbled into ashes, and the door behind it closed slowly and then disappeared. The fires sizzled out.

Merek glared at Todd. "Be more careful!" was all he said and moved on down the tunnel.

"Did you see that?" cried Todd, pulling Lucas close to him. "I made my own doorway and almost got myself killed! I wanna go home, Lucas. I'm not the knight-in-shining-armor kinda guy."

"Pull yourself together," whispered Lucas, shaking his friend. "If we don't do this, we're not going to make it back alive."

"Oh, why did I ever get involved with you in the first place?" mumbled Todd, using Lucas's arm to pull himself up. "Monsters, girls from the past, crazy old men, and me doing magic. We ain't in Kansas, Toto. We friggin' ain't even on the same continent as Kansas."

"Come on," said Lucas. "And like the old man said, 'Be more careful!'"

Merek led the boys through several more tunnels, some sounding so close to monsters on the other sides of the stone walls that the rock shook. Sometimes the light in their path was bright and, at other times, so dim that one could barely make out the turns of the passage. It wasn't long before the three stopped.

Lucas could hear a purring in his ears, but the sound seemed to come from inside his head, rather than from the tunnel. The sound was soft, and the melody was something he'd heard before...no, he *hadn't* heard it before...but it was still familiar somehow. He couldn't explain it.

"I hear something in my head," he whispered, stopping to concentrate on it.

"Yes," said Merek. "The White One sings to us."

Listening more closely, Lucas heard that the man was right. The sound was not purring, but singing—a gentle beckoning song of some sort he'd not heard before. He couldn't understand what was happening, but he felt less fearful and he wanted to just relax and hear more and more.

"I hear it, too," said Todd softly. "But how come it's in our head and not out here?" He motioned to the tunnel around them, being careful not to swing his arms up, thus making another dreaded doorway.

"The White One is speaking to us through our minds. The White One does not need to speak out loud. The White One is powerful." Merek moved on. "The White One will soon be with us."

The singing in their heads was now quite loud, but not unpleasant. It was not a voice—exactly. It seemed a combination of all the good sounds Lucas had ever heard—or never heard. He watched Todd swaying to the song, then noticed that he too was feeling the gentle motion.

Merek stopped and raised his hands to make a new doorway.

This new passage emptied into a brightly lit room. Lucas looked about but could not see the source of the room's glow. There was just light. And that light came from nowhere—and everywhere.

"You have come," said a soft voice inside his head. Lucas's eyes darted around the room but saw no one.

"Yes," said Merek out loud. "It was a long journey, but I have found you again. And I have brought the chosen one and his friend. They found me in the dark wizard's hall. I was chained."

Lucas continued to look around, but still saw nothing. "Do you see anybody?" he whispered to Todd.

Todd shook his head from side to side, also peering about.

"Where is the White One?" Lucas asked Merek. "Is he invisible?"

Just then, Lucas saw movement from a ledge high on the stone wall of the room. Something white was visible one moment and then disappeared. Lucas shook his head and blinked his eyes. He'd seen something, but what?

The White One reappeared in front of him on the floor.

Lucas screamed and fell back against Todd knocking both of them to the floor. "No!" cried Lucas. "I can take anything! I can take the monster in the Black Place, I can take the evil of this Dark Family—I can even eat ratburgers! But I...Can't. Take. A snake!"

A giant white snake was coiled in front of them, strange blue eyes soft with understanding. The upper part of its body hovered in the air at Lucas's eye level, like a cobra might with its invitation to hypnosis. It was not an average snake, however, for the eyes held compassion.

"Do not be afraid of me," a voice said in Lucas's head. "I am the White One."

Lucas sat frozen in his spot, terrified by the white thing before him.

"Okay," said Todd. "This is it. I can't take anymore, either. What we got here is a telepathic snake. We are truly in the *X-Files*."

The snake seemed to ponder Todd and then a voice could be heard in Todd's head. "We have no time to speak lightly. We must save your lives—

and Anitra's, and those of the world. Let us go now."

The voice also told Lucas, "Your fear of snakes will be gone now and never appear in any of your other lives."

Lucas blinked and relaxed.

The snake slithered forward and wrapped itself around Lucas's upper body, leaving its head rest on his shoulder.

"Let us leave this dirty place now," the voice in their heads suggested.

"A mind-reading snake," said Todd in a disbelieving whisper. "This is insane. And my partner—who has been afraid of these slimy things since birth—has a white one perched on his shoulder like a parrot."

The voice inside Todd's head said, "We are not slimy."

Todd looked at the White One from the corner of his eye and nodded. Who was he to fight with a telepathic snake?

Now that the three travelers had found the White One, their passage went smoothly. Finally, they came to a wall, damp with dripping water.

"The moat is beyond us now, on the other side of this wall," said Merek. He raised his arms and waved, making a doorway to the outside world. The moat lay at their feet and they stood solidly on the ground outside the castle.

"What's that?" said Todd, pointing fearfully into the murky water. "I saw something big swimming in there, and it wasn't a goldfish, I can tell you that."

"Moat mambas," answered Merek. "They keep the peasants and townsfolk from crossing over."

"Who would want to cross over to get in here?" asked Lucas in wonder, his eyes glued to the water.

"Many who hate the Dark Family would do harm to the castle and to the evil people inside. They would chip away at the stone to let out the evil stored inside. They believe that the Creator of magic would then destroy this evil, and the castle would fall, killing all inside. That, of course, would be too easy. This is not the case. The people are superstitious."

"And we're not?" remarked Todd. "Well, whatever, I'm not going into that water, Bubs. I've seen too many movies about moats and the things they hide."

The voice of the White One came into their heads as it slithered to the ground and into the water. "Come. If you believe you have the power to cross unharmed, it will be so."

Merek started across the water behind the snake and both arrived safely on the other side.

Lucas and Todd stood watching. Merek and the snake had moved through the darkened water as though they were walking through a kid's swimming pool. No fear, no trouble.

"Ain't no way," said Todd. His feet were planted solidly on the brown grass at his feet.

"We have to," said Lucas. "It's the only way." He paused, took a breath, and then said, "I believe. Look what I did to the chains back in the castle. And look what you did with that doorway. We have the power, Todd. Come on."

Lucas waded out into the moat and moved to the far shore. Todd hung back but finally took a step into the dark wetness. A huge fish with fangs like a dog popped out of the water and snapped at the air in front of Todd's face. He fell back onto the dry ground.

"Okay! All right! That does it! Not me! I am not stepping foot in this moat, guys! Build me a boat! Surely with all the magic goin' on 'round here, you can build me a boat..."

Just then a fierce roaring animal could be heard on the other side of the castle wall. It sounded bigger and louder than the dragon-like thing he'd faced earlier. Todd glanced back quickly. "No, no, no...this can't be happening..."

"That was one of the dark wizard's devils. It will find you and kill you if you stay there by the castle wall. Come; it will be safe. Swing your arms as you did in the tunnels! You will send the moat mambas away!" Merek demonstrated. "You are magic, dear boy!"

Looking skeptical, Todd swung his arms. The moat, at first filled with the nasty fish-like creatures, separated, making a pathway through the shallow water for Todd. "I do believe in magic; I do believe in magic; I do, I do, I do believe in magic," he whispered, a touch of insanity glinting in his eyes. But then he pulled himself to his tallest frame, sucked in his breath, and walked across the moat, strutting like a proud lion. He was magic. Merek had said so.

Once all were safe on the other side, the White One spoke again in their heads. "The evil ones are breaking through now. They know we are here. We must hurry so that they cannot follow. They must not know where we go."

The small group began to run through the fields and into the cover of the forest. The snake had again coiled itself around Lucas's body. Once they were deep inside the forest, Merek slowed and took the snake from Lucas. They moved away from the two boys and seemed to communicate among themselves for a time.

"Can you believe all this?" asked Todd. "I mean, talking snakes and monster fish and all this weird stuff? This would make a heck of a book report. Of course, no one would believe us. Hell, I don't even believe us."

"Don't I know it," agreed Lucas. "You know though, I was scared back there. But I felt this kind of power surging through me at the same time. Did you feel it?"

"Yeah," agreed Todd. "Especially when the Great White Slime came on the scene."

A voice came to Todd's head, "I am not slimy."

"Watch that snake," suggested Todd in a whisper. "It eavesdrops."

Lucas laughed, a little uncomfortable at the notion that the White One could read all his thoughts and memories.

A moment later, Merek and the snake returned to them. "We will go to the house of the Light Family now. It is not far. We will find the dagger, and you, young Lucas, will see Anitra."

Lucas took his breath in sharply. Anitra! He would see Anitra again!

"Steady, pal," said Todd. "Don't forget that we gotta get home...this ain't all about 'getting the girl.'"

The group started on the journey to the Light Castle.

11

ABRACADABRA

The monster floated and watched from the Black Place. For the first time, it felt something akin to fear—a horrible biting horror that ate at its inner evil. The plan was clear to it now. The boy had gone back to the day of the beginning. Back to the time of the wedding. The boy planned to kill Lord Gunnar.

If that happened, the monster would never exist or have a future. It would never float nor eat again! All would be lost.

Was that a good thing? The monster could not remember for sure. Would it die if Gunnar died? Were they not the same being? Yes! Lord Gunnar was the monster! And if the boy killed Gunnar, the monster would die. But then it would never be able to change back to human form to marry the girl and save the family. It did not want this to happen. This could not happen!

It floated and watched as two boys, an old man, and the great white snake escaped the Dark Castle. His family of that time had allowed them to get away by not seeing the importance of the visitors. How could they not think that there would be a Light Family plan for the day of the wedding? Stupid!

If his sister had been smarter, this never would have been possible. Oh, how he wanted to kill her at this moment. Oh, how he hated his sister, Drucil. But now, he had to just wait and hope she would not get in Gunnar's way.

The monster thought and thought. There had to be a way for it to stop the boy so that he could not cause trouble at the wedding. The crack in the Black Place was bigger now. Not by much, but a little.

The monster knew that it could not fit through into another time, though it had tried and tried to squeeze in. It floated back and forth in front of the crack, thinking and thinking, hoping for a plan to spring to mind.

The boy had to be killed before the wedding. If the boy was dead, the girl would marry Gunnar—she would be forced to—and the monster would be human again! But how could it kill the boy? How from this prison it was held within?

An idea sparked and flared.

Yes. It could not go to fight the boy itself. The crack was much too small. But it could send demons from the Black Place to kill the boy wherever he was—living beings created to amuse it in all the lifetimes of waiting! Horrible, disgusting, living things! Wonderful fiends! The boy would die! The girl would be Gunnar's! Why hadn't it thought of this before?

The Light Castle appeared warm and inviting—despite having the same cold stone walls as the Dark Castle. Even so, Lucas felt strange inside, as though there was something terribly wrong. He glanced at Todd, who also wore a worried frown.

"I sense that you feel something odd," the voice of the snake said inside their heads.

Both boys nodded and continued to stare at the castle.

"I feel it, too," added Merek.

"The danger is not there yet," answered the snake. "It comes from the Black Place very soon."

Lucas and Todd looked at each other in alarm. This was not something they wanted to hear.

"Can that monster get through?" asked Todd.

"No," replied the snake. "It has something else in mind."

"What?" asked Lucas.

"We will not know until something happens. Remember, that it sees all except the far future. It will not be happy with the turn of events. I am sad that you did not kill it in the Black Place."

"Kill it! We were lucky to even get out alive," cried Todd, his eyes wide and accusing. "Ya know, we might look like heroes and all, but we just go to school and work the summers in a hotel back home. This whole monster thing is new to us. And magic is not all that easy to control, either, if you want to get right down to it."

Lucas nodded. "I sorry, but I have to agree. We don't like any of this much because we're not good at it. We don't know how to act. How to make the right decisions..."

"How to talk to a snake..." mumbled Todd.

The snake remained silent.

As they looked at the castle, the great draw bridge began to drop.

Lucas held his breath, knowing that Anitra would soon be there with him, and with her, some of his inner strength would return. He was sure of it. She had that effect on him. He felt he could move mountains—or castles—with her at his side.

The difference in the white and dark castles was so evident to the boys now that they stood on the bridge. While the dark bridge had planks missing and creaking hinges, this one felt secure and was well-maintained. Looking over the side, there was no moat, just lush grass and farm animals. It was all very peaceful.

"Lucas!" Anitra cried, and ran to him with open arms, once the bridge was in place. "I was so worried! I have lived my entire life from birth praying that you would be safe and would come for me!"

Lucas held her for a moment and then pushed her back to gaze into her eyes. It seemed just hours ago he had been with this girl in the Black Place, but to her, sixteen years had passed since their last meeting. This was all so strange.

"I marry tomorrow, Lucas," Anitra said. "Have you got the dagger?"

"No, granddaughter," interrupted Merek. "We have not. It is time for the White One and the Elders to sing the song to the Creator. Then the dagger's location will be known to us. Take your friends to rest, and we will call for them when the time is right."

"Don't you know where the dagger is?" asked Todd to Merek. "I thought you were waiting for us!"

"We were," replied the snake. "But the Creator will not speak until the song is sung. You have passed the time when the dagger was buried. Therefore, we do not know its whereabouts. This information was not passed down. The answer is in our souls. And our souls are known only to our Creator. We will sing for the location of the dagger. Go now so that we may work."

Lucas nodded and without further questions, followed Anitra into the castle courtyard.

Todd, trailing behind, said, "I don't think I'll ever get used to hearing that snake in my head. This is insane."

"You said that once," reminded Lucas, taking in the scenery inside the castle walls. "This is surely different from the Dark Castle courtyard. The people here look happy, and all the stalls are full."

Tod shook his head in agreement and looked around. "It smells nicer, too. In fact, it reminds me how hungry I am. And look at all this cool stuff!"

"The difference between good and evil," explained Anitra. "Come inside. Eat and then rest. The next two days may be difficult."

The boys shook their heads as they took in the sights.

"If you don't mind," began Todd. "I just need to sleep right now. I'll eat a little later. I know I said I was hungry, but I can barely stand up, I'm so tired. I'm not used to all this intrigue."

"This is fine," said Anitra. "I will take you to a soft bed. Sometimes, sleep is the way to bringing back a rested body and mind. I pray you have no dreams at all."

Later, having shown Todd to his sleeping quarters, Anitra and Lucas walked the halls of the Light Castle, hand in hand.

"So much has happened to us," said Lucas. "I wonder if I'll ever really believe all this."

"Lucas, you won't have to believe much longer."

He looked at her in question.

"You will forget all this once you go back to your present," she explained. "You will remember some, I'm sure. The hypnotist, for example, since that was part of your doing in your own time. But the dreams will begin to fade, and your traveling from the elevator will have never happened.”

“But I don’t want to forget!” cried Lucas. “I don’t want to forget you!”

“Don’t worry,” she said soothingly. “I will always be there.”

Suddenly there was a crackling noise—loud—and coming closer from the end of the winding hallway. Anitra and Lucas frowned at each other in question just before a bug the size of a dog scampered around the corner. It stopped and stared at them with beady ember eyes.

“I give up,” whispered Lucas, standing still as a statue. “What is that? Some kind of devil-roach or something?”

“It’s from the Black Place! Run Lucas!” She was already steps ahead of him.

He turned and began to run, but no sooner than he’d taken his first, panicked steps, several more of the huge bugs turned the corner and began chasing after them.

“They’re gaining on us!” yelled Lucas. “What do we do? What magic works on them?”

“I don’t know!” cried Anitra. “Fighting things from the Black Place is very dangerous, as you well know! They might be poisonous or they just might eat us!"

The bugs, looking very much like fat cockroaches, scurried down the hall, rapidly gathering the speed needed to overtake them. They rubbed long antennae together and whipped them out toward the runners. One was close enough now to bite down on the back of Lucas's foot. He let out a yelp and turned, kicking out at the bug. He sent it rolling into the other ones and took up running again, blood seeping from his heel.

The bugs pushed around and over the fallen one and resumed the chase.

Finally bursting into the main hall of the castle, Anitra screamed for help.

Within moments, the White One, coiled and ready to spring, stopped the bugs in their tracks with merely a savage look. Its blue snake eyes held them in a trance until, finally, the bugs, croaking and wheezing, started to move backwards away from the white snake that danced in the air in front of them. A gyrating motion kept them hypnotized.

Lucas stood for a moment, frozen in fear, but then stepped forward, next to the snake. He raised his hands in the air and thought of fire, then dropped his arms. His eyes flared.

The bugs burst into flames and turned to ashes before his feet. A loud roar of anger came from another place—the Black Place. And then the air held nothing but silence.

The snake's voice sounded in Lucas's head, "You have accepted the power of the family now. This is good. It will be needed during the challenge at the wedding ceremony. But beware. These monster insects have come from the Black Place. The monster, that was once Lord Gunnar, will try to destroy you, if it can. Let us hope that it will fear your power, now that it has seen your bravery. But I think that even with that, it has no choice but to keep trying or perish. Just as is the case for us. Not all our magic will work on all of theirs—and almost none of it works in the Black Place. We were lucky today. They were startled. Go rest." With that, the snake fell back into a coil and disappeared.

"How does it do that?" asked Lucas.

"It is the White One," was Anitra's only answer.

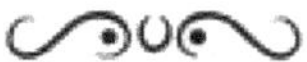

A group of elderly men dressed in flowing white robes, led by Merek, stood in a circle around the White One. The women of the castle stood with small pails of water, just behind the circle of men, every so often offering water to drink.

The woods were quiet. Even the birds were still in the trees above. No insects could be heard. No rustling of leaves. A roar, growing in intensity, filtered through the silence, causing the men to look away from the snake. The sound came from all around them, but no one could identify where it originated.

"Natives getting restless," said Todd, standing to one side of the circle with Lucas and Anitra.

The snake's voice intruded. "The Black Place is getting stronger and the crack larger. The insects were the first, but more terrible things could follow. We need to hurry."

"We feel the need for speed," whispered Todd.

Lucas smacked him hard on the arm. "Is this where the dagger is?" Lucas asked out loud. They'd been standing there looking at the ground for some hours. "I still don't see a thing."

"Yes," said the snake. "It is here finally."

The circle of men opened and the snake's long body slid from a mound of dirt. The golden dagger, its handle jeweled and glowing, sat on the ground for all to see.

Lucas and Todd gasped. "That wasn't there a second ago," said Lucas to no one in particular.

"It has always been there," announced Anitra. "I won't tell you I can explain it all, but it was there. We just could not see it. Now it is yours to defend my family—our family—and our lives."

Lucas stepped forward with caution and picked up the weapon, feeling its strength immediately flow from the handle into his body. He jumped and his eyes grew wide. Looking up, he saw a smile on each man and woman's face.

A pale glow encircled Anitra as though she was an angel. She looked more beautiful than he'd ever seen her.

Todd's eyes were wide, too, for this was of high strangeness.

I don't believe this, Todd said to himself. Then to Lucas, "Look at yourself! Now all you need is to be green."

Lucas, confused, looked down at his body and sucked in his breath. His chest had grown massive, and muscles rippled everywhere he looked. His legs were taunt and strong, and his hands looked worn and powerful. The clothes on his body were stretched to the max, and his limbs nearly busted out of them.

"You have been transformed into the fighter of the dagger," explained the snake. "This is what your long journey has brought you to."

Lucas swallowed and let the dagger hang limp in his hand. He felt like the same person—but different. He smiled to himself.

Todd would laugh at that yet again.

Looking at his friend now, Lucas saw a mere boy. He was small and looked frightened. Yet this was something he was himself only moments before. How strange this world of magic was. It could be so frightening one moment and then so exciting the next.

"The physical magic and the power from the blade only stays with you if you are in possession of the dagger," warned the snake. "This is of major importance: Do not underestimate Gunnar. Should he take the dagger from you when you challenge him at the ceremony tomorrow, he may become more powerful than any of us can believe. Even I, the White One, will not be able to help you if that happens. Take care, Lucas. You hold all our lives in your hands."

Todd and Lucas looked down at the dagger and then back up at those around them. The elderly men and women from the circle, Merek, and the

White One, were suddenly gone. Only Anitra stood near.

"I wish they wouldn't come and go like that," said Todd, breaking out of his surprise of his friend's body changes.

"We must protect ourselves from the monster in the Black Place tonight. It will try again. I am certain. Somehow, I feel it; I know it," said Lucas, his voice clear and precise.

"Whoa, partner," said Todd. "Your voice is sounding just like one of them! Use contractions much? You sound ultra-weird."

"We are all one of them, my friend," replied Lucas, patting Todd's shoulder and then drawing Anitra to him. "Let us go back to the castle now."

"Not by the disappearing act, I hope," mumbled Todd. "Abracadabra."

12

THE EGG

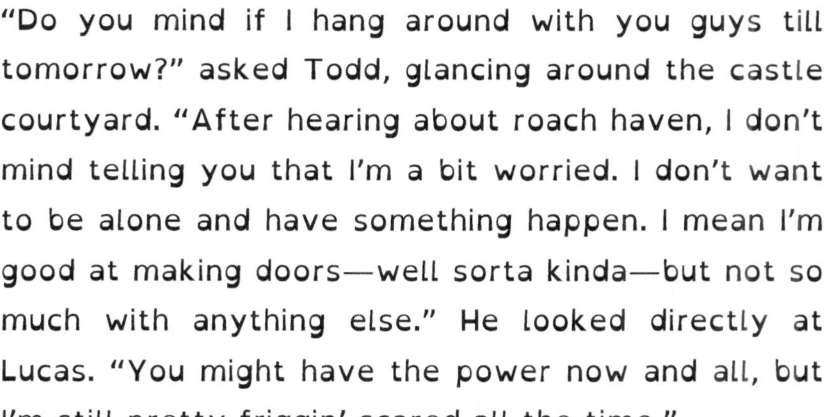

"Do you mind if I hang around with you guys till tomorrow?" asked Todd, glancing around the castle courtyard. "After hearing about roach haven, I don't mind telling you that I'm a bit worried. I don't want to be alone and have something happen. I mean I'm good at making doors—well sorta kinda—but not so much with anything else." He looked directly at Lucas. "You might have the power now and all, but I'm still pretty friggin' scared all the time."

"You may stay," said Lucas. There was no discussion, just acceptance of the circumstances.

Todd frowned at his friend's change of personality. It was disquieting, and made him unsettled, as though he were waiting for the next shoe to drop—rather the next awful thing to happen.

"Please try to understand, Todd," began Anitra, "this is another life belonging to Lucas. You are not part of it in this reality. You are here by coincidence. He is different here—but the same."

"Uh, huh. Different, but the same. Seems like I've heard that one before. It's okay, though. I'm getting used to it, and I'm hangin' in there." Then he mumbled, "No other choice..."

Anitra smiled at him and kissed him lightly on the cheek, making him blush fiercely.

"Believe me," Todd said in a sweet out-of-character voice, "now, I really do understand him wanting to spend every lifetime with you. Got any sisters?"

"Let us now find something to eat," suggested Lucas. "I am very hungry."

"Good idea," agreed Todd. "I'm so hungry I could eat a...a...a rat!"

All three laughed.

Out in the forest, near the Light Castle, the egg gently rocked. It was a large egg (as eggs go), and the color was odd. A greenish tint flowed through a yellow background on an oval shape that looked to be the size of an ostrich's egg. There were tiny vein-like cracks on it that made it appear as though it would break at any second. And, in fact, this was the case. Writhing movement inside was causing the egg's rocking. Something was trying to get out.

In another moment, the egg split open and a black, unctuous slime oozed out of the crack. Little by little, pieces of the egg were chipped away by tiny claws from the inside. And soon, one great red eye appeared. It studied its surroundings from the confines of its shell, the eyeball moving quickly in all directions, scoping out the woods like a hunter. Satisfied that it could come out safely, it quickly broke the rest of the eggshell and popped out.

The creature changed from a single eye to a small black ball, round and smooth with four claw-like hands and one hole—presumably a mouth. It began changing immediately.

Slurping and popping sounds coming from the ball frightened the birds in the trees above, sending an army of flying jets into the air.

Very soon, a fang filled mouth appeared on the ball, just before it burst open again, revealing a silky smooth baby-like creature, its hair now shed onto the ground. The same fang filled mouth remained. The baby grew with alarming speed, cracking and smacking, as well as burping black liquid from its snarling mouth.

Before long, a full-grown adult-sized killer danced about and laughed in the forest, happy to be thriving in the light. It was neither male nor female, animal nor vegetable. It was monstrous.

But coming from the Black Place, this was to be expected. It started to look at its surroundings, oh so happy to be alive. And to have a job.

The monster in the Black Place was pleased. Its killing partner, sent to the past to ruin the boy's plan, was now born to the forest. It laughed and danced and played. The killer would do anything for the monster. The monster had given it life and this gift would be repaid a million times if that were the monster's wish.

Though the monster, itself, could not squeeze through the crack into other times, the small egg slipped through very easily. The killer inside the egg would not fail as the insects had. It would lure the boys with a false face. It would kill them! It would eat them! They would not see it coming.

Stupid, arrogant boys. Though the monster would have preferred the meal not be given to the killer, there was nothing to do about it. That loss would have to be absorbed. The time was speeding by and the boy had to be killed before the marriage. If not, all would be lost. This time, the monster would have its way!

The monster floated and waited and watched. It wouldn't be long now. Not very long at all.

"It is so difficult to believe that tomorrow brings such fear," said Anitra, squeezing Lucas's hand as they walked. "The forest is so beautiful, and the day is so bright. Tomorrow seems far away."

"Yes," agreed Lucas absently, looking over his shoulder to see if Todd was still tagging along.

The three walked deeper into the forest together, enjoying what little time was left before the dreaded wedding ceremony.

Todd hung back from the couple, feeling awkward and in the way. He was too afraid to stay back at the castle alone, though, and being in the company of the White One gave him the creeps. Who made friends with a telepathic snake anyway?

Though Lucas saw how he felt, it was becoming harder for Lucas to understand him and who he was. Strange diction aside, there were other differences, too. Lucas was losing the memories of who he was in *their* time. This was strange—no distressing—but he could tell Lucas felt happy, and that probably had to do with the girl. It was always about the girl. Life in general was about the girl. He only hoped he'd have that kind of luck one day.

A crackling of leaves off to his left caught and held his attention. He stopped, glanced toward the sound and then toward Lucas and Anitra, who was a bit too far ahead by now to suit his taste. Just before calling out to his friend, Todd looked again toward the crackling and saw movement. His skin turned to gooseflesh. Maybe he wasn't as magic as Lucas, but his warning system could still kick in. Something was about to happen. He just couldn't tell if it was good or bad.

The killer's ugly image behind the tree faded into that of a lovely young girl. This was its magic: illusion. And so easy to find what a young boy might want in a world like this. Just a gentle, telepathic touch to this one's brain, and the killer knew what the trap would be.

Luring this boy would be easy.

The plan was then to take them one at a time. It would delve quickly into their minds to find their deepest desires and then become those desires—until they died. Which would be quick...and torturous.

A beautiful girl stepped from behind the tree. She wore a flowing, pink-flowered cotton-like dress that touched the ground. It was low cut in the front and in the back. She held a finger to her lips to silence Todd should he wish to call out, and then she giggled, beckoning him toward her.

Todd glanced toward Lucas and Anitra and then back to the girl. For an instance, a flash of something he could not explain passed the corner of his vision, and his brain seemed to snap in a way that felt almost like a warning. Something ugly. A second later, however, he was looking at the pretty girl again, the creamy softness of her skin, the warm blue of her eyes...He couldn't tear his eyes from her. She was so beautiful. Then he squinted his eyes and frowned. Was something off?

She gestured again for him to come to her, giggled once more, and then skipped off, looking back to invite a chase. Her dress hung off one shoulder and the long skirt rustled as she ran.

Todd licked his lips, looked cautiously after her and then walked toward the girl. Part of him wanted to go the other way, but there was something holding him hostage. He felt like he could not turn or even look away. It was as though she had tendrils pulling him forward. But there were no tendrils. Just a warming voice in his brain that spoke of love.

She stopped running when he hesitated, licked her lips, and held out her hand to him.

Taking small steps, the nearer Todd got to her, the faster his heart beat. A flash of something not quite right always seemed just outside his vision but he had difficulty honing in on it. Something kept tearing it from his mind.

He stopped though and took a step backwards. He wasn't a movie buff for nothing. *They always getcha when ya least expect it*, he thought. This was a don't-go-into-the-basement-you-fool kind of moment if there ever was one.

The killer saw that its prey was not falling into the trap in the manner it had hoped, and because of its intense anger, the thing from the egg lost its concentration. The full power of its ugliness shot forth, knocking Todd to the ground.

Todd opened his mouth to scream, but nothing came out. Somehow, with its ugly power, the creature held him so tightly in an invisible cage that he could not move, and the killer was nearly upon him! Gone was the luscious lure, replaced by evil born of the Black Place. He knew now that he'd made a terrible mistake, and it might very well be the last he ever made.

Always a sucker for a pretty girl, he thought. *I gotta get a handle on that. If I ever get the chance again.*

A bolt of lightning shot over Todd's head; Lucas was by his side, the magic dagger pointed straight out in front of him. The next bolt coming from the dagger hit the killer directly in its face.

Black ooze poured out before its entire body exploded. The remnants of the egg monster pooled on the ground and then sunk into the earth. In seconds, it was like it had never been there.

But for Todd, the memory was all too fresh. He'd nearly been killed. He lay panting and shaking on the ground as Lucas leaned down to help him up.

"Are you all right?" asked Anitra, pushing Todd's fallen hair from his eyes. "Why did you go off alone like that? You could have been killed!"

"I'm...sorry." Todd struggled to calm himself. "I felt in the way following you guys and then I saw this pretty girl...Only it wasn't a girl. It was something from the Black Place, wasn't it? Don't answer. I know it was."

"Yes," replied Anitra.

"It is gone now," said Lucas, looking around the area to see if there were other creatures about. "We have defeated the monster's plan again. I will be glad when tomorrow has come and gone."

"I'll be glad to go *Back to the Future* again," said Todd, brushing off his clothing. "Or the present. Or whatever..."

"You've never really been in the future in the first place. Not from this point, anyway. That would be still another timeline," remarked Lucas in his old fashion.

Todd jerked his head up, recognizing the playful tone, but the old Lucas was gone again, replaced by some new character. He sighed. No matter. Lucas was Lucas. Whichever life. His friend.

A shiver chilled Lucas as he looked once again at the Dark Castle, this time from the safety of his white stallion. The White One, coiled around his waist with its head up above his shoulder, spoke quietly inside his head.

"The challenge must be made before the wizard has a chance to use any form of black magic to dull our senses. I will, of course, attempt to use my own magic, but I cannot be sure of the wizard's power inside the Dark Castle. It will surely be stronger than mine, and my magic will then be of little use to you."

Lucas nodded and the White One continued, "There is more at stake here than you know. Much more at stake than the lives of Anitra, your silly friend, and you. There is much evil in the world of the future. You must know that by now. It comes from many beliefs and the arguments over who is right."

Lucas frowned, not understanding.

"There are many religions, yes? And each has its own beliefs. Each also has its own kind of evil trying to banish the good of others and to overtake those not of their same beliefs. This causes resistance to the abundance of all." The snake's tongue darted, smacking Lucas on the cheek with a sting. "Are you listening, boy?"

Lucas nodded again, trying to understand while rubbing the swelling spot on his cheek.

The snake, hissing, seemed angry now. "The world does not need to add this particular evil to the others. This Dark Family is too strong and could destroy the world. If the monster ever leaves the Black Place, the world, as you know it, will end. The great apocalypse you've heard of will be your only reality. This must be stopped now. It will make the stories from your Bible that the present Lucas believes in—those of Revelations—a quick truth to be reckoned with. The union between Anitra and Gunnar will not be as the Creator planned in the beginning. The Dark Family has become strong enough to fool even the Creator with its scheming and elusive lies."

The White One paused for a moment before adding, sadly, "And our light magic will only dull their dark magic the tiniest bit. Still, that small bit will be acceptable to the Creator for the smallest bright spot in evil is a good thing. However, the Dark Family will be free to release evil throughout time. They will never stop until all time and all beings are their slaves inside evil.

"This cannot happen!" the snake said, squeezing coils tight about Lucas's waist. "You must show the Creator now, in this time, that the evil in Gunnar is too great to be released on the world—even with our Anitra at his side."

Lucas raised the glittering dagger and looked at it. "Will this dagger be strong enough to save us all?"

"It must be," replied the snake. "It must be."

The rotted drawbridge loomed before them now, and an armed escort rode out on black horses to take the Light Castle wedding party into the courtyard. Once inside, Lucas, dressed in the same long concealing white robes as the others, fell to the back of the line. He did not want to draw attention to himself before he was ready to make the challenge.

Todd's white robe had a baggy hood that fell over his head, hiding most of his features. This was necessary since there had been no physical change for him. Gunnar would recognize him as the jester immediately.

Anitra, dressed in the white wedding gown of the time, looked radiant but held a sad, frightened posture. She already knew the outcome of another lifetime. The last time, there had been no dagger. She had run away with Lucas, leaving Gunnar behind to become the monster in the Black Place. That could not happen this time.

Gunnar would die—or Lucas would.

Anitra held her fear at bay. She didn't want to feel selfish, but it was difficult to consider what would happen to her if Lucas failed and she was forced to be the wife of the monstrous Gunnar. Thoughts of escape were already burning in her mind. Yet she pushed them away, knowing that her family would suffer the consequences of her deceit should she not follow what was meant to be.

Gunnar and his sister, Drucil, greeted the group, offering each a goblet of dark liquid.

"Do not drink it," the snake's voice said to Lucas. "The others must show a false face and take the drink, but not you. Pretend. It is surely laced with magic potion."

Lucas raised the goblet to his lips and pretended to drink, then cautiously poured the liquid at the base of a vine growing up the courtyard wall. The vine shuddered and Lucas held his breath, hoping no one had seen the plant's odd behavior. It would not be too difficult to see that the vine had tasted the drink and not he.

The snake seemed to wink. *Is that possible?* Lucas thought and then smiled.

One by one, members of the Dark Family, ugly and evil, paraded out of the castle to welcome the Light Family. It was strange, seeing people who could not, or would not, smile. Their faces looked sinister and twisted, and it was difficult to look at them without cringing.

Yet they were happy. He could tell, and that in itself was disturbing beyond his way of thinking.

Soon the two opposing households stood facing each other with Anitra and Gunnar in front.

Gunnar reached out for Anitra's hand, his deformed face quivering in delight and Anitra's twitching with disgust. She too was feeling the plight of not being able to look at the monster in front of her. "Let the ceremony begin," yelled Gunner, holding her hand high in the air for all to see that he held it.

"Wait, my brother!" said Drucil. She was pointing at the hooded boy near the back of the White group. "Is that not the jester? The one we chased through the tunnels?" She marched to Todd and ripped off his hood. "This is all some kind of trick! Kill—"

"Stop!" interrupted Lucas, stepping forward and raising the dagger to the sky.

"I challenge you, Lord Gunnar! You may not marry Anitra! She is mine!" Lucas's voice rang like a ceremony church bell over the crowd—loud, clear, and demanding.

For a moment, the entire crowd stood silent, frozen by the abrupt end of the ceremony. Even Gunnar, powerful and evil in his own home, was dumbfounded.

"I accept your challenge," said Gunnar barely above a whisper, hate pouring from his eyes. "I accept it!"

The monster in the Black Place roared in anger! But all it could do was float.

13

THE DAGGER

Lucas and Gunnar stood facing each other; one with a very special dagger and one with no weapon at all.

Lucas hesitated, and the snake spoke inside his head. "Do not feel ashamed that you have the dagger and he carries no visible weapon. The dagger is your strongest magic. Gunnar has his magic inside him, and he does not fight fair. You should be wary of that and give him no advantage. You will find that evil will cheat whenever it needs or wants to. This is powerful evil you face, boy."

Gunnar laughed at Lucas's indecision and threw off his cape. His body was as well developed and as strong as Lucas's. The match would be equal in strength.

He pointed his finger at Lucas; fire leaped from it, outward toward Lucas's eyes.

Lucas fell back, covering his face with his hands, barely hanging on to the dagger. The pain shot through his head.

"Touch the dagger to your eyes," the snake's voice ordered.

Lucas quickly did as the White One said; his vision cleared and the pain disappeared.

Gunnar sent more fire his way, but this time Lucas fell to the ground and rolled, jumping up and swinging out with the dagger. He sliced at Gunnar's boots, leaving smoke to trail from the sizzling leather.

Gunnar cried out, but rushed at Lucas again, this time using both his hands as weapons.

Lucas dodged, and the flames, missing him, blazed fire to a Light elder standing near. The man screamed and fell to the ground. Without thinking or care to his own safety, Lucas jumped at the elder and touched the blade of the dagger to his body. The fire went out and the man sat up, showing no signs of being burned. Even his white robe looked untouched.

The man nodded his thanks to the boy, but the dagger could not take away the weakness caused by the fluid the man had ingested, for that was magic of the most evil kind. He could not stand by Lucas.

Gunnar and Lucas faced each other again, both now realizing their powers were equal.

Lucas seemed to remember someone somewhere saying that evil could always win unless good was very, very smart. He hoped he was smart enough.

They each circled, looking for an opportunity to strike a deadly blow to the other—one that would disable the other enough to make a final thrust of power to win Anitra.

Something popped into existence between them. A large monster insect, from the same family as Lucas's earlier attackers, prepared to pounce. It was bulkier, and the teeth more intimidating, than those prior bugs. It moved closer to Lucas, and he held out the dagger to stop it.

But the dagger did not react. There was no lightning or brilliance of any kind.

Lucas fell back.

Within seconds, the White One was coiled in front of Lucas, ready to protect him from the insect, which was now scampering forward, its poison teeth chomping air.

"The dagger chooses when to kill and when not to. There is a reason for this!" The snake's voice whispered inside Lucas's head. It sprang forward at the bug, biting it, and killing it before it had a chance to use its poison fangs.

Gunnar took the moment to move past the bug and snake and throw his leg under Lucas's, knocking him to the ground. Lucas's dagger flew from his hand and landed in front of Gunnar's evil sister, Drucil.

Lucas, without the dagger, turned back into the boy he had been before. He lay helpless on the ground, his breath ragged and his heart pounding in fear.

Gunnar, standing tall, laughed at Lucas. He threw patches of fire all around the boy's head, while the Light Family stood back, unable to move to help. The liquid they had taken earlier still held them in a weakened state, and they could be of no aid.

The White One, however, raised its body to strike.

"Stop, great snake!" ordered Gunnar. "Or I'll kill the boy right now! Then I will take the dagger and kill you, too!" He left Lucas and walked to the dagger. Drucil and Gunnar bent to take the weapon together, their eyes locked on each other in triumph.

The White One, still coiled on the ground, began its song to the Creator.

A burning and crackling could be heard as the two Dark Family members grasped the dagger at the same time. Both families stood silent, not knowing what to expect. Even the dark wizard, who had been ready to cast the spell of death on the White One and Lucas, stood motionless.

Drucil and Gunnar looked into each other's eyes for one long moment, the knowledge of the ages holding them silent. The dagger held secrets that they should not have taken. Had they known, they would not have rushed forth to steal it from the boy. They should have never touched the dagger.

In that instant, a howling from the Black Place pierced their minds and all became clear to them. They knew why they were there and how the Black Place worked. They knew who was in the Black Place and why. They knew that their time of power and magic was over. They had failed their family.

Gunnar clutched the dagger and his sister's hand, looking up to grasp a moment from the eyes of his beloved Anitra. Time froze for this encounter. He sent a false longing to lure her in the final seconds of his life, stilling the cries of agony in his mind from the black thing in the place beyond—the thing that he knew was a rebirth of himself. All Anitra need do now was have a shard of pity for him. All she need do was step forward and touch him ever so gently. All she need do was forgive.

He could see, however, that this was not going to be his fate. He'd not thought it possible, not from his sweet Anitra, but a hatred bubbled in her eyes as she gazed back at him. A hatred so vile that his heart jumped at the wonderful prospect of its very evil.

But in that same instant, that look of malice was gone, banished as he had been all those lifetimes ago to the darker place of the world. She was pure again.

Still, she would never touch him with the kindness he needed to remove him and his family from their deaths. The Creator would not ask this of her again.

It was then that he looked back to his family about him. Not one of his own had come to his defense. Evil themselves, they would not—could not. Watching pain was too seductive for them.

And so, they, too, would move from this time and place. He watched his family turn to ash, falling to the ground in heaps about the courtyard. In moments, the ashes were taken by the gentle winds.

And then it was his time, though he separated himself from it by escaping through the tiny crack into the Black Place—joining his evil monster self, stilling the beast's cries of loathing and fear of no longer living to hate. He watched, from a distance it seemed, his sister's flesh fall from her body, turning to liquid on the ground, sinking into its depths.

Gunnar reached forward and called the liquid to him, sucking in the evil she had been and cradling it in his black heart. He refused to watch or feel his own end, his rotting away into food for the ground creatures. Yet, as much as he resisted, he could feel the nothingness overtake him, the monster in the dark place careening down and down and away...

The crack closed. Gunnar was gone. The monster in the Black Place was gone.

The White One slithered over to the dagger sitting in the ashes of the Dark Family and coiled itself around the jeweled handle. A smoky film of ash still covered the blade, a remembrance of the darkness in the world and the need for the recognition of evil by any name.

"The dagger was a power of good from the Creator," said the snake. "I have sung the song and given back the evil so that the Creator can disburse it in the heavens and turn it to good. In the hands of the Light Family and its hero, Lucas, the dagger was a powerful weapon. In the hands of evil, it destroyed the user by a mere touch. The moment Gunnar and Drucil touched the blade, they were lost. The dagger will be buried again."

The snake and the dagger disappeared, but a voice still sounded in the heads of those looking on. "Until it is needed. When it is needed."

Lucas turned to Anitra and ran to him. "You did it! You saved our lives! The monster in the Black Place is gone because Gunnar is gone! By touching the dagger, he took his own life! Now you can return!"

"I don't want to return, Anitra. I don't want to leave you," said Lucas softly.

"You must. It is the way of the time. We will meet again. I promise you!"

In a blink, Lucas and Todd found themselves on the floor of a foggy elevator. They looked at each other with alarm and confusion. Lucas's eyes finally softened and he let out a breath. "Wild ride," he whispered. "I think we're back," he said calmly to Todd.

"I should hope so," replied Todd. "Did all that really happen? Maybe it was mass hysteria. Mass meaning you and me. Did we eat some bad burgers?"

Lucas squinted. The fog was clearing in the elevator, drifting off to the ceiling and through cracks in the machine's workings. For a moment, he remembered something about a girl and a dagger, but the thoughts were slipping away. He glanced back at Todd. "What did you say?"

Todd sat on the floor and frowned. "I forget. Why are we on the floor?"

"I remember going to a hypnotist," said Lucas, a memory sparking. "Something about a past life. There's a recording of the whole thing in the car."

"So?" answered Todd, standing and brushing off his jeans. "That stuff happens all the time."

"Yeah," said Lucas thoughtfully. "It does."

The elevator doors opened.

A lovely girl carrying a white cat stood in front of them, an amused smile on her porcelain face.

Lucas blushed.

"Do you always sit on the floor of an elevator?" asked the girl.

"No," said Lucas, hopping up. "I think the elevator jolted or something...and it jerked...and we kinda fell...or something..."

Todd, still feeling confused a bit, just looked at the girl and her cat. "Your cat is staring at me, Miss."

"Anna," she said. "My name is Anna." She turned the cat towards her and spoke to it in baby talk, "He does that sometimes, doesn't he? Pretty little White One." She looked back at the boys and then said to the cat, "Aren't they silly boys?"

Lucas was having trouble taking her eyes off the girl, and Todd was eyeing the cat as if it were ready to pounce.

The girl said playfully, "This is my cat, White One. Do you like cats?"

Lucas smiled widely. "I love cats," he said ushering all of them out of the elevator. "But I hate elevators."

"You hate cats," whispered Todd, nudging Lucas in the side. "You're allergic."

Is that purring in my head? Lucas thought. An odd sensation. It was like something soft was rummaging around through his brain. It was crazy.

"Take my word for it, I love cats now," replied Lucas, looking at the girl of his dreams. Could any one girl be that beautiful?

Todd shook his head and the cat winked a blue eye at him.

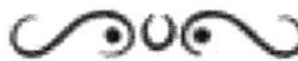

A new lifetime? Or an old one? In a world plagued by evil, there's always one more monstrous tale to be told...

EPILOG

ANNA

Arlin watched from the top turret window of the castle. The Dark Family was being destroyed by a stranger, and the wondrous girl everyone had been talking about—the one who would save their world—stood meekly by. It was all such a sickening regret. The Dark Family didn't need saving. They just needed new management. No luck there with all of them dead. *Except for me*, he thought.

He'd been banished to the filthy hole of a place at the top of the castle weeks ago by his mocking Uncle Gunnar. There'd not been much food since then, and he was losing weight and brain power because of that thankless fool. Soon his magic would begin to slip if he didn't get out, and 16 was too young an age to just let it all go. If he didn't think of something, he'd really be in a witch's pot of trouble—or dead. He couldn't live without his magic—didn't even want to. The problem was that there would be no one now to visit him to deliver meals to keep death from happening. He'd be locked away, it seemed, forever—until ending and collapse—if he didn't figure out what to do next. He'd been forgotten.

Punishment was hard in the Dark Family, but this sentence had not been warranted. He could not help that he was the only one in the entire family who had a pretty face. Truth be told, it had helped, out in the natural world. It made his life easier in some ways. The obnoxiously good people would follow him—not knowing that he was sucking them dry of energy—because that's what he did. That's what he was. An energy vampire.

Inside the castle walls where evil mostly looked evil, no one really knew what he was capable of. He was just what they called "pretty evil." And the majority was disgusted by it, thinking it was not up to their standards of viciousness.

That wasn't true though. He could do much worse. Blood and guts were not the only measures of evil. His abilities ran toward the silent and still, yet as massive in outcome, but not so clear of intent early on. But he'd done nothing wrong to warrant banishment to the towers. His uncle had merely been in a bad mood, and he'd been there to receive his anger.

Mother Drucil had not cared one way or another. He was an embarrassment to her, and she hadn't even considered him her son. To her, offspring were only valuable if they had good built-in skills or were truly evil in ways that would bring her glory. She just didn't understand him.

So, he'd made sure his glory was his. To hell with them all. He didn't share any of it with any of them. How dare they mock him because he was beautiful and they were ugly? He had more abilities than they would ever understand.

Arlin was one who hated his own kind. Oh, he hated those different from him, as well. In other words, he hated most everyone. He was the living dead.

Well, no matter now. The dead told no tales he'd not already heard. No good ones, anyway. He laughed out loud, watching the last of the ashes of his people float into the skies. Then he watched the family of Light move away. They'd not seen the last of him. He hoped.

Now he needed a plan. He laughed again. Make no mistake, Arlin was evil and mean and every bit as vicious as his uncle, but he was not nearly as fast in the thinking up of plans department. That might prove to be a problem. He sat on the floor with his back leaning against the cold stone wall to consider his next steps.

Anna took in her breath casually, sitting across from the two boys at the local diner. It took everything she could muster not to throw her arms around Lucas and tell him how much she loved him. But she couldn't do that.

Things had happened much too fast. There was supposed to be a time of lull when everyone could gain their senses after the destruction of the Dark Family. The family could gather themselves and plan out what the future should bring. Everyone had seen the destruction of the future where she and the boys had visited to get away from the monster in the Black Place. This strange world should not have existed. Their world should not have ended that way.

That had to be stopped and be closely considered. Why had the devastation of that timeline taken place and then led to something looking like nuclear destruction at the place she and the boys had seen in the future? It was a bad omen to be sure.

Sitting there, knowing the issues and the mystery surrounding it, made things even more difficult. There was no one to confide in, as such a confidence was something that had led to the last set of difficulties. She wanted to tell Lucas what was happening, but that would put his life in danger again—as well as his friend, who she'd come to care greatly about.

The danger was a surety. The great White One snake from her past gave one final warning before leaving her in this world and changing its body.

The danger is not over, it had said inside all family heads. Be vigilant, be brave, and be smart.

Cryptic to be sure. The great wizard, Merek, had said that it could be no other way if the snake had not known the exact manifestation of the danger. It only knew that there was more to be done to make the worlds safe. And in that instant, she'd materialized in the hotel lobby of the Bellington, just seconds after Lucas and Todd had been pushed back to their world.

She'd not had time to think about any of it, only had time to look down at the great White One now with her—a beautiful white cat. At least he was with her as advisor. That was something new for her. Welcome assistance.

She looked down at herself, half-heartedly listening to Todd talk about a hypnotist and how it had confused their minds. Wearing tight black leggings, an oversized colorful shirt, and strange mesh shoes, she barely heard him. Her cat was in a carrier, small and petite, with the White One looking out with big eyes. He did not look happy.

Her attention snapped to the cage and she noted that the White One was gone. Then Todd mentioned another life for Lucas in an small village. That was something she knew about. Had Lucas remembered it?

Lucas was nodding, "Yeah, it sounds strange, but it really did feel like I was there. The doc said it was past-life experience. Can you believe that?"

Anna smiled at them, more disappointed than anything. "Yes, I do believe in that kind of thing. There's been a lot of research into it, and the human condition is much larger in the universe than anyone ever thought." It was not a real remembrance, but one pulled from a medical professional. It would not help matters now. She did her best to hide her disappointment.

"I just don't know why I feel so weird right now," said Todd. "It's like there's something at the edge of my brain or on the tip of my tongue that I need to remember, but it keeps slipping away."

"Yeah, me too," added Lucas and then he looked directly at Anna. "Then you showed up with your cat—where is he by the way? Anyway, it was like that was supposed to happen. Feels like something left undone...Feels like I know you..."

"The cat's sitting out in front of the hotel," offered Todd. "It's like he owns the place."

Anna laughed, shifting in her seat, and kicked the carrier where the White One had been just moments before, further under the table. "That's like the White One, of course. He does act like he owns everything. And actually, if I'm totally honest, he really does."

Lucas and Todd glanced at each other because her words felt real and not just good-humored.

"So," she said, steering the boys from more discussion about the great White One, "do you work at the hotel all the time?"

Again, they glanced at each other.

"Well, just for the summer. We work the elevator." Lucas nodded.

Both boys frowned.

"There's something about that elevator though..." said Lucas.

"Yeah, it's crazy complicated," said Todd. "It does more than go up and down..."

"Oh?" Anna asked softly. "Whatever do you mean? How can it do more than go up and down?"

Lucas coughed. "What he means is, that it's old and there's been something wrong with it or something...It's nothing." And it truly was nothing for as long as they chose to talk about it, the less they remembered.

Anna looked out the window to see the White One bounding across traffic to get to the diner. The cat was jumping over the tops of cars, not worrying about what people would think about that or whether it was in any danger. Then she felt it, too. Something. Nothing. A bad thing was coming.

She lurched up from the table. "I'm sorry, I've loved talking with you both, and I hope that I can see you again soon. But I have to go right now. I've forgotten something important!"

"Ain't we all," whispered Todd with a frown.

Then she rushed from the diner and was gone.

The Black Place was silent. But that didn't mean that it wasn't thinking and moving and planning. It was true that it did its best work when a monster flowed about its halls and rooms. But it didn't really need anyone or anything to keep it dark, vicious, and reaching for murder.

A place could be evil.

Now it played in the empty space. How nice to have slimy floors and change them to tar in the blink of a bloody eye. Well, of course, there was no actual eye. But the place had memories and replaying them was an ideal way to move its days and nights forward. The monsters who had come to live inside its home over the eons all thought it had been they who had made the varied horrendous visual effects. And, true, the ideas had often come from them, but it was the place itself that made those events happen. It had been the prime inspiration of its own wishes and addictions that forced it all to occur. That was what made it worthwhile.

It fed on the fear of trapped visitors and roared with 'happiness' when those guests died at its whim. It had seen the death of children and animals and stupid adults who thought that they had the control. It bellowed with silent laughter.

Control.

What did any of them know of the wonderful influence of evil? How could they possibly mimic any kind of pleasure when the Black Place was swirling though the vast number of worlds, stopping and starting as it chose? Killing and torturing at its leisure.

Evil places were everywhere.

For some reason it, had stayed in this same place of the prior monster. That monster had vanished, as often happened when losing a battle to the good—when they stopped listening to the wise place and took it upon themselves to do their own dirty work. Their mistakes often multiplied, and their defeat became evident. Still, the place had always moved on to new horrors when that happened.

But not this time. This was a first. It stayed in place.

Was another monster coming so soon? The place, though suspicious, was a bit pleased. What role would it play? After all, it did enjoy the company of monsters.

Getting to know them was like raising an evil child. A vicious, gleeful sound erupted within the silent space. It did long for the day when its halls and room would spread across the worlds without judgment—when every corner would welcome it ...and goodness would be ousted forever.

For now, though, it would sleep until awakened. Until it was needed. It was sure that this would take place very soon.

NOTE FROM AUTHOR

The fascination of the elevator in a special hotel began for me in the early 1980s in the lovely town of St. Petersburg, Florida. Visiting a writer's convention one summer, I had the ideal opportunity to spend several nights at the Princess Martha Hotel—or at least I believe it to be that hotel, since it was a long time ago, and my memory for the details outside the grandness of the place and my own limited research may have been lost at this late date.

Inside the hotel, there was an elevator. Yes. *The* elevator. There were no scenes or fog inside it, but it was the old-time kind of contraption that I've used in this novel, with a lever and an actual elevator attendant to take you up and down from your floor to the beautiful spacious lobby. I was so interested in this elevator at that time but had not a clue why. Then over the years, thinking of it often, and of the varied elevator boys on summer jobs who took me up and down for that week-long stay, a story was born.

I found an old newspaper article from not too terribly long after my stay that told of the hotel going into federal bankruptcy, and it seems that now (at the time of this writing) it has been turned into a retirement home. If you search the Internet for it, you will see from old postcards that show just how grand this 1920s structure was.

I wonder if it's haunted? It has to be, right?

END

www.ingramcontent.com/pod-product-compliance
Lightning Source LLC
Chambersburg PA
CBHW061300210726
48293CB00003B/1050